ANYTHING BUT YES

ANYTHING
BUT
YES

A NOVEL OF
ANNA DEL MONTE,
JEWISH CITIZEN OF ROME,
1749

JOIE DAVIDOW

Monkfish Book Publishing Company
Rhinebeck, New York

Paperback ISBN 978-1-958972-08-3
ebook ISBN 978-1-958972-09-0

Library of Congress Cataloging-in-Publication Data

Names: Davidow, Joie, author.
Title: Anything but yes : a novel of Anna del Monte, Jewish citizen of
    Rome, 1749 / Joie Davidow.
Description: Rhinebeck, New York : Monkfish Book Publishing Company, [2023]
Identifiers: LCCN 2023006993 (print) | LCCN 2023006994 (ebook) | ISBN
    9781958972083 (paperback) | ISBN 9781958972090 (ebook)
Subjects: LCSH: Del Monte, Anna--Fiction. | Jewish
    women--Italy--Rome--Fiction. | Jews--Italy--Rome--History--18th
    century--Fiction. | Catholic Church--Relations--Judaism--Fiction.
Classification: LCC PS3604.A94535 A85 2023 (print) | LCC PS3604.A94535
    (ebook) | DDC 813/.6--dc23/eng/20230412
LC record available at https://lccn.loc.gov/2023006993
LC ebook record available at https://lccn.loc.gov/2023006994

Book and cover design by Colin Rolfe
Cover images: "Rêverie sur le Seuil" (1893) by William-Adolphe Bouguereau
"La via Rua, il fondo il Portico d'Ottavia" (1888) by Ettore Roesler Franz

Monkfish Book Publishing Company
22 East Market Street, Suite 304
Rhinebeck, NY 12572
(845) 876-4861
monkfishpublishing.com

Blessed art thou, oh Lord, our God,
King of the Universe,
who has returned the soul to its body,
And allowed the blind to see.

PREMESSA

TO THE *Kind Reader:*
The Jews of Rome have lived behind ghetto walls since 1555, when, in his first year on the papal throne, Paolo IV, terrified by the Protestants and desperate that Catholicism should remain the one true church in Europe, wrote his infamous bull:

"We declare it absurd and utterly inconvenient that the Jews, who through their own fault were condemned by God to eternal servitude, residing in a place where Christian piety allows them access to our society, are so ungrateful that instead of thanks for gracious treatment, they return invective, and instead of the servitude which they deserve, they claim superiority. They dare not only to live amongst the Christian people but also in the vicinity of the churches and even in the most noble streets and squares. They wear no identifying garments, buy and hold property, engage maids, nurses, and other Christian servants, and commit numerous dishonorable acts without shame and in contempt of the Christian name."

So it was decreed that until the end of time, in every city within the Papal States, Jews should not presume in any way to work, eat, or fraternize with Christians. That we should live in enclosed streets, separated from society. That we should have only one synagogue in each city and should construct no new ones, nor should we own buildings or land.

Forced to sell whatever properties we owned at whatever price we were offered, six hundred Roman families moved into this new Jewish quarter on the swampy banks of the Tiber River, where we rented any shelter we could find at whatever price the Christian landlords chose to charge us. To add to our suffering—and increase our outrage—we were taxed to pay for building the walls that enclosed us. All the synagogues, apart from the one allowed, were destroyed. Sacred texts were confiscated and burned. From seven synagogues, we were confined to one, the Cinque Scòle, a single building with a single door, in which we devised separate spaces for congregations with differing rituals.

Within our ghetto walls lived families who came in refuge from Sicily, Naples, Spain, and Portugal. And Jews who have lived in the city since the beginning of the First Roman Republic centuries before anyone heard the name Jesus Christ. We have been scholars, doctors, jewelers, and traders. During the reign of Julius Caesar, we were senators.

My honorable family has lived in Rome for three centuries. We were bankers, among the wealthiest in Rome, but since 1682, when the Jews were deprived of banking licenses, we have been forced to earn our living by dealing in old things. Jews are banned from every guild, every profession, and every faculty of every university, save the faculty of medicine, and even there, we are barred from the ceremony when degrees are bestowed for fear we will contaminate the good Catholics.

The Church, ravenous for mass conversion, assumed that

in our suffering, we would forsake the faith of our ancestors. But we did not. So succeeding popes used other means to persuade us, taxing the very clothes on our bodies. And as even that failed, they tried to convert us through both punishment and reward, offering money and professions in exchange for our souls.

Their greatest prize was the soul of a young woman, innocent, without guile, too used to the protection of her father and brothers to resist threats of baptism or eternal hell, a woman young enough to bear many Christian children with the gentile they chose for her husband. One such woman was my sister, Anna del Monte, may her memory be a blessing.

In 1749, something barbarous took place at my house. A certain person, may his name be erased from the Book of Life, converted to Catholicism for the sole purpose of striking at the soul of my honorable father. Armed with two lying witnesses, he presented himself to the vicegerent, at that time Ferdinando de' Rossi, claiming he had been inspired to become a Christian and wished to share the Catholic faith with the woman he called his bride, Anna, daughter of Benedetto del Monte. Seeing that the claim had been certified by a notary, the vicegerent sent an order to the pope's sheriff, the bargello, to transport my blameless sister to the Casa de Catecumeni where she could be properly interrogated.

This bargello, Giovanni Sguazzi, was an arrogant man and a virulent enemy of our Jewish nation. No sooner had the order been received than he asked his informers about our family, and discovering that the del Monte were highly respected and as prosperous as a Jewish family could be in the misery of our circumstances, he planted himself at the door to our home, pistol in hand to prevent anyone from entering or leaving, and demanded to see the memunin, *the ghetto's governors, at that time Samuele Corcos, Moisé Modigliano and Angelo Zevi, who is the brother of my honorable mother, may her soul be bound in eternal life. When they arrived, he informed them of de' Rossi's order and threatened them with arrest if they failed to deliver Anna at once.*

So few who are taken ever return that none of us knows what becomes of them. My blessed sister recorded a diary of those terrible days in her own hand so that a record might survive of the trials she endured. She hid the diary at once since accusations against the Church are punishable as heresy.

After she went to her eternal rest, we thought we would find the diary among her possessions, but we searched every corner in vain. We would have asked the great Rabbi Moisé Mielì, who might have received the diary, but just as we were about to approach him, sudden death severed the thread of his life. His papers were left to his half-brother, the Most Excellent Rabbi David Calò of blessed memory, and then to their brother Abraham Elia, an insipid fool, who sold the precious archives of his most wise brothers to Caciaro de Segni, who bought paper by the pound. One day, this de Segni randomly dared to read some of the papers and, realizing that he had found the much-desired diary, ran to my sister Allegrezza and told her that he had paid one baiocco for it, which I quickly repaid.

You cannot imagine the tears of bitterness I shed when I read the sufferings of that most pristine soul while she was incarcerated in the despised Casa de Catecumeni. In these tumultuous days, as a new republic is born, and we dare to hope for relief from the hardships we have endured, I have transcribed her story, not motivated by pride but to preserve her memory and in the hope that those who suffer similar trials will bear them in peace, knowing that God protects the innocent.

As I write these words, nearly five thousand souls are locked in a ghetto of one hundred buildings on three hectares. We have closed into ourselves, like fingers making a fist, and made of this crowded prison a haven, our miqdash m'at.

My dear readers, if you are curious to know what Anna del Monte endured from the time she was taken by force, I invite you to read the following pages.

—Tranquillo del Monte, Rome, February 1798

ROME

O NE BELL. One hour after dawn. The light of a Roman April rouses the narrow ghetto streets. From balcony railings, worn garments in harlequin shades of red, violet, blue, and green wave like flags in the warm morning breeze. On the Strada della Rua, a merchant arranges baskets overflowing with used bits and pieces—tableware, kitchen utensils, doorknobs, drawer pulls, hinges. Half-hidden in his doorway, a jeweler sits at a table covered in worn black velvet, arranging and rearranging his display of coral and silver.

Stray cats chase each other through the rubbish and shadows of the alleys down to the Strada della Fiumara on the banks of the Tiber where the air reeks of fish and feces. Ancient stone houses slump shoulder to shoulder like drunken old men, every decrepit room, every stifling attic, every dank cellar, home to five or six people.

Women carry chairs out into the street, maneuvering to find a shard of sunlight. Graying heads bend low, nose to fabric, so that ruined eyes can see tiny stitches. Calloused hands mend a linen tablecloth, reline a jacket, add fresh lace to the ragged hem of a skirt. One of the women is nearly bald, another's neck is gnarled by a goiter. Most of them are missing teeth. A woman wheezes, shoulders rising with the effort of each breath, then coughs violently, lungs clogged with lint and dirt. Even the youngest of the women looks old. They are the daughters of Zion, descendants of Rachele, Ester, and Miriàmme.

On a rotting wooden landing near the Arco di Azzimelle, a woman stops beating dust from a rug and leans over the railing to berate the ducks, goats, stray dogs, and naughty boys who are causing a commotion in the alley below. At the Piazza delle Tre Cannelle, a plump grandmother staggers from the fountain, a full bucket balanced on her head. And in the tiny Piazzetta del Pancotto, the aroma of freshly baked bread breezes about, momentarily cloaking the stench of the public toilets.

Near the Piazza delle Cinque Scòle, elegant English gentlemen in search of souvenirs use silver-tipped walking sticks to poke through crates of cheap treasures—a mosaic rendering of the Coliseum, a fragment of marble statuary scraped and pounded to appear ancient. Ladies examine etchings of squalid streets made quaint, holding the cards away from their faces with gloved fingers.

Just outside the Gate of Severus, four guards, young and muscular, joke and laugh, kick the cobblestones with the tips of their boots, adjust the pistols lodged in their belts. While on the other side of the gates, street peddlers wearing the yellow caps that mark them as Jews throng the Piazza Giudea, their wares tied up in bundles or piled onto pushcarts. They wait impatiently, indignantly, not daring to raise their voices. This is an old game the guards are playing, dawdling past the hour when the heavy iron bars should be lifted, the gates opened.

ONE BELL. One hour after dawn. On the *piano nobile* of the Palazzo Della Ospizio Apostolico, the Most Illustrious Ferdinando Maria de' Rossi, Archbishop of Tarso and Vicegerent of Rome, kneels on his prayer bench. He wonders if his purple skullcap, his embroidered silk cape, the gem-encrusted cross that rests on his frail chest might really bring him closer to the ear of the Blessed Virgin. He looks up at her portrait, clasps his hands as tightly as he can, and begs her to remove his doubts, to assure him that what he must do today will satisfy the will of God, and not merely the petty appetites of small men who imagine themselves powerful. "And remove the veil from the hearts of the faithless Jews," he whispers, "so that they may acknowledge Jesus Christ our Lord. Do not exclude from thy mercy even Jewish faithlessness: hear our prayers, which we offer for the blindness of that people, through our Lord Jesus Christ, Amen."

The second son of a Florentine marquis, Ferdinando Maria de' Rossi was sent into the Church, like so many aristocratic second sons, so that his older brother could inherit the family estates intact. He has been compensated with a lengthening string of honorifics—Vicariate, Bishop of Boiano, Patriarch of Constantinople, Dean of the Tribunal of the Apostolic Signature of Grace. Armed with unwavering tenacity, exceptional intelligence, and a gift for flattery, he has climbed with sure feet nearly to the rank of Prince of the Church, but he has reached the age of fifty-three, and the cardinal's scarlet *biretta* remains beyond his reach.

The vicegerent's father, Marchese Pietro Paolo de' Rossi, left the education of his sons to the strict teachings of the Jesuits, and the raising of his daughters to the careless attentions of the servants. In the evenings, as young Ferdinando climbed the curving marble staircase to his bedroom, generations of cardinals looked down on him from gilt frames—an uncle, a great-uncle, a great-great-uncle, all princes of the Church. His own future was never in question. While his older brother was groomed to manage the family estates, he was sent to the Jesuit Collegio Romano, then to the university at Macerata for a degree in *utroque iure*, canon and civil law. He was soon given a position as honorary prelate to His Holiness the Pope Clemente XII. And he had a protector, Cardinal Federico Marcello Lante, whom he cajoled and flattered like a devoted lover, never failing to demonstrate his gratitude.

The *vicegerent's* sharp eyes discern whom he should adulate, whom he should ignore. He imagines his portrait in the red robes of a cardinal hanging beside those of his ancestors. It ought to be there now, but he has been too closely aligned with the Jesuits whom the pope deeply mistrusts. He hopes that he will outlive this pope and that the next pope will mistrust them less.

De' Rossi has made enemies. He has been outspoken at times when a more prudent man might have held his tongue. He has been accused of seeking favor, of unbridled ambition, but he thinks these accusations are unearned, leveled at him by colleagues who are no less eager for their own advancement.

With each title, he has acquired an additional source of income. The room in which he prays is large and lavishly furnished. The chairs are upholstered in silk velvet, the tables varnished with gold, the bed hung with tapestries, the floors covered with Persian carpets.

He opens his eyes and gazes at the Madonna who looks down from Piazzetta's painting, smiling gently. If what he must do is not God's will, if it is unjust, even cruel, he is not to blame. He will be forgiven.

ONE BELL. Anna thinks the bell tower must be straight over her head. The sound clatters the earthenware jug on the food chest, vibrates under her feet. She sits on the straw covered plank, adjusts her shawl to cover her collarbone, winds her long auburn curls and secures them to the top of her head with her silver pin.

Last night, when the *sbirri* pulled her out of the carriage, the prioress was waiting for her, smiling as though she were welcoming a guest. She pressed Anna's hands, promised that she wished only to care for her. Then she brought her to this cell and locked the door behind her.

Anna had been at home, working in the kitchen when the sbirri pounded on the outer door, the thunder of the pope's blackguards come to seize the presumed guilty.

Last night she slept fitfully on the wooden plank, a thin straw pallet with a rough woolen blanket. She attends to herself, to a dozen little wounds, runs her fingers over the scratches on her back where the straw of the mattress poked through its thin covering, examines the bruises on her arms where the sbirri's rough hands gripped her as they hurled her into the carriage waiting just outside the ghetto gates. She hadn't dared to undress. Her skirts are crumpled, the laces of her bodice undone.

She has nothing to do here, so she waits. Waits to hear the footsteps in the corridor, the rattle of the prioress's key ring. In the eighteen years of her life, she has never been alone, never slept alone, never eaten alone. Her legs tremble beneath her skirts.

She wonders if all nuns live like this, caged in desolate cubicles. She has seen flocks of them in the ghetto, hidden in robes of black or gray like visions from another time. They paw through baskets of used pots and pans, examine the fabrics in her uncle's shop, always looking for a flaw, always asking for a better price. But until she met the prioress, she had never spoken to one of them.

She searches for something pleasant to soothe her weary eyes but finds nothing. The lime-washed walls are streaked yellow with moisture. A single barred window offers sparse light, but no trace of sky. It frames a brick wall so close she could touch its surface if she were a little taller and her arms a little longer. The bricks have been patched and replaced, century after century. Modern bricks, pale in their newness, long flat bricks from the time of the empire.

A chair stands stiff and unfriendly beside a table whose surface is thick with decades of wax, veined with the scratches of a thousand nuns. Last night, the prioress left a bit of bread in the wooden food box and a jug of water. She asked Anna what she would like to eat, but she cannot eat anything here. A boiled egg, she said. And prayed it would be a kosher egg without a trace of blood.

⁓

TWO BELLS. Two hours after dawn. The ruby and diamonds in the vicegerent's ring leave trails of light on the polished top of the mahogany table as he gestures to one of his *auditori,* then to another. He asks, "Who was sent?"

Four young Jesuits nervously finger the wooden crosses that lay on their breasts. The secretary who answers is eager, always the first to speak up.

"Giovanni Sguazzo, Your Excellency. The bargello himself went, taking with him four men and a carriage."

"Squazzo!" de' Rossi grimaces, both horrified and amused. "The bargello delights in delivering misery to the miserable. It must have pleased him greatly to humiliate a family such as the del Montes."

"Yes, Excellency," the young man nods, not because he is in agreement but because it has never occurred to him to question the opinions of his superiors.

The vicegerent sits back in his chair, folding his hands. The acquisition of souls is a difficult business, and the bargello will have handled it badly. "I suppose Squazzo has submitted his report?"

"Yes, Excellency."

Again, last night, Vicegerent de' Rossi was unable to sleep. He is too tired to be patient, too anxious to wait for a written report. "Relate it to us, will you? Who among you is prepared to do that?" He glances around the table, but the same, eager young priest has already begun to speak.

"Excellency, two of Squazzo's men stood sentry at the door of the palazzo with pistols drawn while the three Hebrew governors were summoned and presented with Your Excellency's order. The Jewess was promptly retrieved and taken to the Casa dei Catacumeni. She has been in the care of the prioress since yesterday evening."

"And there was no trouble?"

"She went without excessive struggle. The Jews ran after the carriage hurling stones, as usual. Nothing more."

THREE BELLS. Three hours after dawn. In the morning light, Anna can see that the pale face of the prioress, corseted in a stiff white wimple, is blotched red and wrinkled, and that the old woman's features are arranged to convey a benevolence she has no reason to trust. The nun is very strange. She is full of good cheer, although she has lived out her days within these walls, dressed in robes that cover every inch of her, leaving only her face and hands open to the pleasure of the spring air. She speaks in the breathy, obeisant voice Anna imagines she must use when addressing her Jesus Christ.

The prioress says, "My daughter, I pray that God may enlighten you and make your heart contrite."

She says it kindly, but Anna is enraged. She has been enraged since the sbirri pounded the butts of their pistols on the door of her home, and she is struggling to stay enraged. The alternative is despair.

"Are you saying, Signora Prioress, that I am not enlightened, that I am lacking in faith? But I will remain enlightened so long as I am not perverted from the holy religion into which I was born. My heart will be contrite so long as I am worthy of the light of our sacred sabbath."

She waits, expecting her arrogance to be met with rebuke, but the prioress chooses to overlook her rudeness and wags her little head, wimple quivering. "My child," she says, "you have only just arrived, and our ways are new to you."

She will refuse to become accustomed to their ways, no matter how long they keep her here. She is imprisoned in this cell. Her jailer, the sweet-faced old nun, says, "I have blessed news this morning. His Excellency Vicegerent de' Rossi will soon arrive to interrogate you. It is a great honor, and you must prepare for it."

Anna forces her lips to smile, her voice to remain calm. "Tell me, please, how must I prepare myself to meet this vicegerent? I was not permitted to change my dress before I was taken from my home and brought to this place. You see me in a soiled skirt, which I wear only to work at home in the kitchen. As I was permitted to bring nothing with me, I have the benefit of neither comb nor mirror nor even a change of linen. I am as tidy and clean as any Jewish woman makes herself in accordance with the laws of Moses."

The old nun's face has become frozen from so many years of compulsory smiling. If she detects the fear behind Anna's proud words, she shows no sign of it.

Anna turns away to hide her expression and examines the wall. The cracks and streaks that mar the whitewash might be a map of the city of Rome. The ghetto might be there, where a long crack ends in a spot of mold.

The prioress says, "You must prepare only to open your mind and your heart to the vicegerent's words."

Anna bows her head, absently fingers her shawl. *P'tach libi b'toratecha … open my heart in Thy Torah, and in Thy commandments let my soul pursue.*

The prioress bows her head when he enters the room, concealing her awed expression. Anna curtseys. His Excellency the great vicegerent is an underfed stick of a man, long nose, thin lips, curled periwig sliding off a nearly bald head, violet skullcap, black *abitocorto* edged in violet. Behind him, a young priest carries in a cushioned armchair, then backs away. And the key turns in the lock.

Do they imagine she will run for the door? That they will have to chase her as she races from this stone convent? Do they really fear she might dash through the streets of Monti where Jews are more despised than in any other quarter of Rome?

Perched on his cushions, the great man seems too small for the chair. He smiles. His teeth are small and straight. "I am Archbishop de' Rossi," he says, "Vicegerent of Rome. The Pope has entrusted me to watch over your people, to care for them. Perhaps you have heard my name mentioned in your home?" He speaks facetiously. Every Jew in Rome knows who he is.

"You need not fear me," he says, assuming that she is afraid of him. He asks her to please sit. The wooden chair is closer to him than she cares to venture, so she lowers herself onto the edge of the bed.

This skinny little creature is the overseer of the ghetto, second in command to the cardinal vicar. They say he has private audiences with the pope every Wednesday and Saturday for the sole purpose of discussing what to do with the Roman Jews.

Stories fly through the ghetto. Waiting in line at the public ovens, filing out of the synagogue, women and girls whisper to each other. If you are locked in the Catacumeni, you must never say "yes," no matter what anyone asks you. Say, "That would be nice," or "please," or "how kind." *Anything but "yes."* You must never admit to any belief, no matter how they try to trick you. Your only defense is to remain silent as long as you can bear it, and if you must say something, it must always be "no." You have only to say "yes" once to any question, and they will be quick to sprinkle you with holy water and declare you baptized.

Anna sees the adoration on the face of the prioress and wonders if she should fear this man. The Jews have their own governors, the *memunim*, but the pope has made this Catholic man ruler of the ghetto. He has the power to release her or imprison her, the power to make life easier for her family, or even more difficult.

She cannot force herself to look at him, but his raiment is exquisite. The lace that spills from his sleeves is astonishing. Many noble garments pass through her father's shop, but she has never seen lace so intricate as this.

She is shabby and unkempt, a disgrace. Her skirt is spotted, grayed with washing, her topknot carelessly wound. Her family wears the repaired and embellished castoffs of the aristocracy, but they are always elegant, never vulgar or overdone. The bodice of her mother's finest gown may have been cut from the silk that once cloaked a duchess, but she is more refined than the richest women in Rome.

Anna is her mother's daughter, a descendant of the

Zevi and the del Monte. She can, at least, hold her body as proudly as though she were well-dressed. She sits erect, feet together, chin lifted. She will give this vicegerent no cause to believe he is dealing with an ignorant ghetto girl.

"Do you know why you are here, my child?"

What a question! Surely, it was he who ordered her abduction.

May God keep my tongue and my lips from speaking slander, and to them that curse me let my soul be silent.

He waits for an answer, but she offers none. He smiles with a closed mouth, thin lips covering his tiny teeth. "This cloister, the Casa dei Catacumeni, is a refuge for those who wish to be instructed in the ways of Our Lord, Jesus Christ. Perhaps you have expressed such a wish."

Baruch atoi Adonai. Blessed art thou, oh Lord, our God.

"Perhaps you have been persuaded that your soul might be saved."

God of our ancestors, God of Abraham, God of Isaac.

"Perhaps there is someone who wishes you to join him in his conversion to our Holy Catholic Religion."

God of Sara, God of Rivka, God of Rachele, and God of Lea. How she would love to know who turned on her. What spying, jealous liar gave her name to the Office of the Inquisition?

"Perhaps a young Christian has become enamored of you."

"No, Your Excellency, I am innocent."

"Dear daughter, you must not be ashamed to tell me the truth because this is universal among unmarried girls, as common among the Jews as among all the others, and you are no different."

She thinks he must know that he is insulting her.

"No man can boast of having spoken with me, neither in my home, nor outside it, nor can he boast of having seen me at a window talking with a living soul. Our custom is different from that of your gentile young people. Our unmarried girls never go out. So, I ask Your Excellency to understand that I cannot have conversed with any man."

He nods, pushes his boney body out of the chair. If these were his only questions, why has he come here? To have a look at her? To accuse her?

He says, "I will pray for you, dear daughter. I will pray that God might enlighten you."

And she is alone in the cell, standing at the window, searching for the sky. The colors of the brick wall are richer now, cognac, port and claret, but the cell is still grim and barren. She closes her eyes to comfort herself, imaging carpets on the floor, paintings on the walls, soft cushions on the rigid chair. She has learned more from the vicegerent than he has from her. Is a young man in love with her? A young man, he meant, who has denounced her, a convert, no doubt, who swore he heard her say something, anything, that might suggest she wanted to become Catholic. But who? Who has made her the victim of his shabby revenge? Has her father refused to employ someone? Offended someone? Who could have seen her? She never leaves her home alone. She rarely leaves it at all. She goes out only to attend services at the synagogue, climbing a few steps to the *matroneo*, where unmarried girls sit on long benches behind married women.

From the balcony, they peer through iron grating at all the proud splendor an oppressed people can muster—walls covered in damask, draperies embroidered in

scarlet and gold, intricately filigreed silver incense burn-
ers, brimming oil lamps engraved with the words "Holy
be the Lord," each precious item marked with the crest
of the family who provided it. Her ancestor, Jakov del
Monte, donated the silver Torah crown studded with
gems.

Dressed in the finest clothing their families can afford,
the young women whisper behind prayer books, sharing
gossip about the cousin who has become engaged, the
brother who has finished his apprenticeship. Crescenzio
has grown handsome. Salomone has grown fat. They
start to giggle, and one of the married women leans back
and angrily motions them to shush. Anna respects the
Torah. She loves it with all her heart. But the sabbath is
a holiday.

Through the iron grill that hides them, the women
watch their fathers, brothers, husbands, and sons on the
floor below, wrapped in fringed white shawls, swaying
in prayer. Sometimes the melodies fill Anna with joy.
Sometimes she is a little bored. But when one of her
own, her brother, father, uncle, cousin is called to read
the Torah, she smiles and listens, and the married women
turn to her, nodding.

Lately, she has been watching her brother's friend,
Gabriele Sereni, watching his soft lips move as he prays, his
dark curls bounce as he bends his head, watching the way
he walks, listing a little when he is called to the *bimah*. He
cannot see her, but she can see him perfectly. She still sees
the little boy hidden inside his manly body, the squeaky
laughter in his deep, rich voice. When they were small, she
watched Gabriele and her brother chase each other. When
they became young men, she watched them walk home

from the *yeshivot* carrying books, arguing, discussing, and she tried to hear what they were saying. She wanted to tell Gabriele that she knew things, read things, that she could argue as well as her brother. But she and her sister Allegrezza were in the kitchen with Mammà, straining to hear Tranquillo and Gabriele in the sitting room discussing the meaning of the weekly Torah portion.

There were times when she answered Gabi's knock at the door, times when he greeted her with a smile, times when he patted her head, or said a few words to her before Tranquillo appeared.

Then the day came when she answered the door in one of Allegrezza's dresses, her hair braided and wound around her head, and she saw in his face that she had become a woman. He no longer patted her head, and if she met him at the door or passed him in the street, he lowered his eyes.

On two separate occasions, she thought she'd caught him staring at her. The first time this happened as she was leaving the Cinque Scòla, her mother's arm hooked through hers. She felt his eyes, she was sure she did, and she looked up. He quickly looked away, but her face was hot, and the palms of her hands were damp. Mammà didn't notice anything, and really, she had nothing to tell her. But Anna began to watch him, Saturday after Saturday, straining for a glimpse of him through the grill of the women's balcony.

Then it was spring, the month of Nisan, the first full moon after the northern equinox, and every woman in the ghetto was busy with *Pèsechi* preparations. Every year, Anna, her mother, her grandmother, and her sister turn the family's rooms upside down, scrub the cupboards clean, boil the dishes and utensils to kosher them for Pèsechi, just as her great-grandmother and her great-grandmother's great-grandmother did.

They search out every crumb of leavened food and bundle it up for the rabbi who sells it to the goim or feeds it to the geese. They chop vegetables to make *ocam*, layers of chard, spinach and chicken giblets with crumbled matzoh browned in goose fat. They bake almond macaroons, *ciambalette,* and sponge cakes scented with orange peel. Mammà's *stracciatella* soup simmers over the fire. Tatà brings home a freshly koshered capon for the first seder meal.

On the Vicolo delle Azzimelle, the ovens are kept hot night and day. All year, the goim come to the ghetto to buy *pane azzimo,* matzoh flavored with onion, garlic, or herbs to satisfy their Christian tastes. They love matzoh all the more because their Church forbids it. To them, it is a novelty, a treat. But the Jews consider this unleavened bread a sacrifice, a reminder of their suffering on the flight from Egypt.

On the first morning of Pèsechi, as Anna, her sister, her mother, and grandmother were walking to the synagogue behind her father and brother, they came upon the Sereni family, and it was then that she caught Gabriele Sereni staring at her for the second time. She looked up. He held her gaze for one second, two, by the third second, she was no longer breathing, but then his mother fell on her, kissing her cheeks, blocking her vision, and his sister came to squeeze her hands, and by the time they moved away, she'd lost sight of him.

Ten days after the last Pèsechi seder, she was abducted from her home and brought to this abominable place.

~

ON THE night when they came for her, Anna was in the kitchen with her sister and her mother, washing up after the evening meal. The sbirri used the butts of their pistols to bang on the door, over and over again. Every family in the ghetto lives in fear of that sound. If the door is not opened at once, they destroy it. The pounding was a knife in her belly, slicing her apart. Her sister Allegrezza grasped the edge of the table they'd been clearing. The women looked at each other. *It is not for us. They have come for one of the neighbors.*

Mammà put her arms around Anna's waist and held her tightly. Her grandmother, *Savta* Rachele, sank onto the bench and covered her face with her apron. Tatà was already halfway down the staircase.

When he returned, three sbirri were behind him, menacing them all with their pistols. The Jew-hater, Bargello Squazzo, came in grinning, looking all around as though their home were a museum of oddities. Rabbi Mielì followed behind them, breathless from climbing the stairs, and then came the three memunim—Mosé Modigliano, Samuele Corcos, and her mother's brother, Angelo Zevi, who was carrying a document she realized was an order to seize one of them.

Her father and the memunim spoke calmly to Squazzo. They protested, reasoned, covered their rage with false humility, knowing it was useless. Squazzo felt no such compunction to conceal his disdain. He shouted, waved his pistol over his head like a small boy with a new toy, threatening to arrest every Jew in the room.

"Which of these women is Anna del Monte?"

~

SHE HAD barely managed to fall asleep when the heavy wooden door scraping the stone floor woke her. Three priests carrying lanterns entered the cell, Christian soldiers in dark, hooded cloaks wearing wooden crucifixes in place of swords. Three shadows flowed across the walls like a dark river, stinking of sweat and urine.

What can they mean to do here? Will they torture her? Rape her? Who will come to save her if she screams?

She sits up, hides behind the rough wool blanket, thanks God that she had been too afraid to undress before sleeping.

Two of the men are on their knees, mumbling prayers. The third sits on the wooden chair, his dark eyes glowing in the lantern light, a demon whose deranged smile reveals yellowed teeth.

"*Shalom Aleichem.*" Peace be with you, the demon says in Hebrew, a ludicrous attempt at charm. "My sister, I was a Jew like you, and like you, I will always be a Jew."

This putrid demon with dirty fingernails dares to claim that he is a Jew. The body is the vessel God has given us to contain the soul and it is a Jew's duty to treat it with respect. Every morning a Jew washes. A Jew washes before and after eating, and again after touching something unclean. Every week, a Jew goes to the bathhouse to steam and scrub the body.

The priest says, "I have seen the light of truth and left my first religion to become Catholic, to be part of the true faith. I have come here tonight in the hope that you will see the truth through me."

He says that for a time, he preached to the Jews of

Ancona every Saturday afternoon. Anna knows these men, all of them converts who preach sermons Jews are forced to attend. They think they persuade the Jews to become Catholic by littering their diatribes with Hebrew words or, worse, by speaking in the dialect of the ghetto.

No one preaches more spitefully against the Jews than those who have converted, fanatics who first praise then insult them. They rage against their former religion as though they were convincing themselves. No Jew has any love for these traitors. Now she is locked in a cell with three of them.

"When you become a Catholic," he says, "you will become a better Jew. I have tasted the honey in the rock. I have found in Christ the King of the Jews and in the Roman Catholic Church the completion of Judaism. In the New Testament, I have found the fulfillment of the promises made in the Torah. Do you not believe that the Lord Adonai, our God Eloheinu, created Adam and Eve, the parents of all people?"

Does he really suppose she will answer him?

"Do you not believe that Adam brought disaster upon himself through his sin and closed the Gates of Heaven to us all? Do you not believe in the existence of the One True God? You have nothing to say? You do not know the answer? Of course, you believe in one god! In Adonai, in Elohim. And do you not understand that this means there can be only one true religion, one true Church?"

Even if she could summon the courage to speak, she would not answer him. If she answers, if she says "yes" to anything, she will never be released from this place. If she shows the slightest hesitation, the slightest fear, he will see it as a sign that he is progressing in his forced conversion.

There are three of them, and she is only one small woman. She wonders where the prioress sleeps, and if she would hear her cries. And if she heard them, would she come to save her?

Anna begins to hum. While she hums, she cannot speak. *C'era pure Moscé lo ladro ch'arubbava li biscottini. Più n'arubbava, più ne magnava.*

There once was a thief named Moses who stole cookies from the *kal.* The more he stole, the more he ate. There once was a thief named Moses...

The priest pounds his fist on the table, a violent sound like the butt of the sbirri's pistols pounding on the door of her home. He thinks he will terrify her, but he cannot force a word from her or even compel her to listen. She sings out, "There once was a thief named Moses who stole biscuits from the kal." She tries to remember the next line. "There once was a thief named Moses...

"Answer me, daughter of Israel! Do you not believe in the God of Abraham?"

She thinks that she has surprised him by refusing to betray her fear, that his rage weakens him. He leans forward so that his head nearly touches hers, and his male stink is so strong her words are choked.

"Do me the kindness of leaving me in blessed peace. I believe only in what my honorable parents believe. I was born a Jew and I will die a Jew, and I have no wish to listen to your sermon. I beg you to leave me."

He laughs. "I have seen your sort many times, and I have converted them all. I will convert you, as well."

He is just a stupid man, a weak man, a bully. She pulls the blanket away from her face so that he can hear her very clearly.

"You can preach at me as much as you like. It won't matter at all if you preach at me night and day."

He leans back, tilts his head. "You do not wish to hear me? But you will listen. If I had not seen and touched the truth with my own hands, I would not have accepted the Catholic faith. I have come to enlighten you, so that your soul will be saved as mine has been.

"Do you not believe, as the Torah teaches, that all-merciful God promised to send a Redeemer, a Messiah to atone for the sin of Adam, to reopen the gates of Heaven that were closed to man? Do the prophecies not tell us that the Messiah would be born of a virgin, a descendant of King David?"

What defense does she have against this invasion? She can only send her thoughts away from this dark cell, from this putrid priest who never stops spewing his unbridled arrogance. She searches for something nice to occupy her thoughts. When she leaves this place, she will make a new bodice from the bit of sky-colored velvet her mother has given her. She will ask Chiara how she winds her braids to the back of her head.

The priest is pounding on the table again. She cannot allow him to see that the violence of the sound unnerves her. Surely, the whole convent must be awake from this noise.

"You are obstinate, daughter of Israel, unwilling even to answer my questions. You will force me to speak to the pope about you! If you refuse to accept the true faith, you can stay in this cell one hundred years."

Does he think she will believe that the pope himself listens to a lowly convert in a soiled robe?

Depart from me, all you who do evil, for the Lord has heard the sound of my weeping.

TWO YEARS before she was abducted, Anna del Monte attended a Catholic sermon for the first time. Of the four thousand Jews over the age of twelve living in the ghetto, the memunim are obliged to select three hundred in rotation. After services on the sabbath, the day of rest, whip-cracking sbirri herd the selection into the Piazza della Cinque Scòle, then march them through the ghetto and out the gate to the Church of Sant'Angelo della Pescheria. Sbirri walk beside them, ahead of them, and behind them.

Unmarried girls are always accompanied by a parent or close female relative to protect them from the lascivious Catholic men who line the street, hurling stones and insults. "Jews! Dirty Jews! Whores! *Malanno e danno!*" Diseased and damned.

Mammà held Anna by the arm. She said, "Keep your eyes down and put one foot in front of the other. How terrible can it be? Hundreds of sermons and not one conversion."

But it was terrible.

When they arrived at the church, they were counted like goats. Every name was checked off. If someone on the list was discovered to be absent, a rabbi or one of the memunim appeared to pay the fine.

Then they were inspected. A large man in a long

white cassock and a black cloak peered into Anna's ears to make sure she had not stuffed them with cotton or wax in order to avoid hearing the sermon. It took a long time to inspect three hundred pairs of ears.

Slowly, they filed into the church, the women and men together. Mammà looked about frantically for a moment, then found a place for them between two older women, Monnà Modigliano and Monnà Velletri. No man's thigh would touch Anna's, no man's arm would accidentally brush across her breast. Mammà said, "You will do what I do. You will say some prayers in your head. Maybe you will remember a few lines of your beloved Latin poetry. And when it is over, we will go home and take a little glass of wine to cleanse the bad taste from our mouths and our minds."

Anna had never been inside a church. It was much larger than their little scòla but also much less beautiful. Whatever decoration hung above the altar had been covered in cloth. "The *mumzer*, the bastard," Mammà whispered. "A painting of their Christ is under that cloth. They hide it so we will not have to look at it. It is the only kindness they ever show us."

The upper gallery, where the women should have been seated, was crowded with laughing *goim*, shouting, "Stupid Jews! Dirty Jews! Stinking Jews!" Finally, the sermon began, and they fell silent. The preacher must have been a convert. He knew some words of Hebrew and he knew the Torah portion they had heard at the scòla that morning, but he did not know what it meant. He began to describe it, distort it. He misquoted Isaiah. "I have spread out my hands all the day unto a rebellious people who walk after their own thoughts in a way that is not good."

Mammà whispered, "You do not need wax to close your ears." Anna no longer heard the preacher. In her head, she heard, "I lift my soul to you, Adonai; I trust in You, oh Lord. Do not permit me to be disgraced, nor let my enemies triumph over me. Oh Lord, let me know Thy ways; teach me Thy paths." The twenty-fifth psalm. But the preacher became impossible to ignore. He pounded the lectern. He shouted that the Jews were stubborn, ignorant, blind, and the goim in the gallery shouted back their agreement.

Monks patrolled the church carrying long sticks, poking anyone who closed his eyes, stopping anyone who tried to leave. The preacher said that Jews were perverse in their refusal to accept the Savior, that they would all burn in hell for their obstinance. Anna thanked God that she did not have to endure this torture very often.

Now she endures it day after day, hour after hour.

A NNA LAY awake, her arms crossed over her breast, hugging herself for comfort. Every moment, she was afraid that the priests might return. Every moment, she thought she heard a footstep in the corridor, the rattle of keys.

When dawn's light dripped down the old brick wall, her eyes were still open. Fear still raced through her body.

When the prioress came, she found the girl trembling and arranged her features in a mask of kindness. She sat beside Anna on the bed, pressing her hands and looking into her eyes with what passed for sympathy. She made no mention of the demon priests who came in the night, and Anna said nothing to her. Nothing at all.

~

NOW THE prioress has sent three nuns to the cell, two all in white, one with a black veil. They are familiar to her, unmistakable, even wrapped as they are in wimples, like blinders on a horse. The ghetto is a small place, four thousand souls crowded onto three hectares. Anna has seen these women before. Perhaps they lived in the muck and filth of the Strada della Fiumara where the windows open onto the river and the bottom floors are foul with mold. What devil's bargain have they made to trade their ghetto rags for these clean gowns?

The prioress has told Anna that she sent the young nuns to keep her company, but they are either too shy or too frightened to talk. Perhaps they have been forbidden to speak with a Jewess. They kneel on the stone floor, counting off the wooden beads of their rosaries, mumbling in chorus, and Anna wonders if they are praying for her soul, or if she ought to pray for theirs.

ONE SABBATH morning, while she sat behind the screen in the women's section of the scòla, hoping to catch a glimpse of Gabriele Sereni, a girl carrying a newborn baby appeared in the entrance to the sanctuary below, just at the threshold no female foot is permitted to cross. She shouted, "Arone Funari, this is your son!" The pious men swaying in prayer became quiet. The impious men chattering at the back of the sanctuary fell silent. The women on the balcony held each other's hands tightly and stared.

The girl, Gigliola, was very young, no more than fifteen years of age, with the clear unblemished face of a child and unblinking eyes. No one went to her. No one spoke in her defense. Her father, her uncles, her male relatives—where were they that morning?

Rabbi Mielì said nothing. Anna thought he could not speak because he was shocked, but now, as she remembers that morning, she thinks that the rabbi is an old man who has seen many things, and that he was not surprised at all, but too sad to speak, heartbroken even, that such a thing should happen to a Jewish family. After a long moment, the rabbi's eyes began to move through the congregation, like an archer finding his target. Arone Funari pulled his prayer shawl over his face.

"Is this true, Arone?" The rabbi spoke very softly but everyone heard him. As though he himself had been accused, Arone's father said, "Rabbi, the girl must be lying. I have never seen her before. She does not belong to our kal. My son cannot have known her."

For Arone to lie to his father would have been an even greater shame than making a baby with a woman who was not his wife, so he confessed. "Forgive me, Tatà."

The girl disappeared soon afterward. She could be here in this convent, a nun like the three who kneel, counting rosary beads. And the baby? If she brought it here, it would have been snatched from her arms, baptized, and given to a childless Catholic couple.

The ghetto is too small for secrets. Many Jews spoke cruelly of Arone. Many more spoke cruelly of Gigliola, eyebrows raised in disgust, as though such a thing could never happen in their own families.

How did it happen to her? Was her life so devoid of joy that she took comfort wherever she could find it? As for Arone, the rabbi tried to persuade him to marry her. His father tried to force him, and his mother howled that he was killing her with his shameful behavior. But

Gigliola was gone, and a few months later, Arone married someone else, the youngest in a family of four daughters who had such a tiny dowry she could do no better.

~

This afternoon, a man they call the Curate of the Catacumeni has arrived, all kindness and soft talk, a round little *goi* in a black cassock, his rosy face encircled in a cloud of beard. He acts the part of an affectionate grandfather, calling Anna his *amata figliuola,* beloved daughter. "We are all praying for you," he says, "praying for the salvation of your soul."

He says it is his duty to care for all the souls in this place and that it will be his privilege to redeem hers, as though redeeming a soul were as simple a task as rendering chicken fat. He has been telling her his version of the story of Daniel, and she wishes he were more entertaining. She has heard that *parashah*, year after year, since she was old enough to sit with her sister in the women's gallery of the kal, and even before that. She could repeat it to this overfed goi without omitting a single detail.

He speaks softly, bending toward her as though confiding an important secret. Even in the Torah, the story is not a long one, but he embellishes it, comments on it. She tries to pass the time by sending her mind elsewhere. She would rather be in the kitchen with her sister, chopping onions.

This curate speaks of Hanania, Misa, and Azariah, who refused to bow before King Nebuchadnezzar's golden statue. In punishment, they were thrown into the flaming abyss, but they did not burn. The old curate has made a strange choice. What is his point? The Jews refused to worship idols because theirs is a jealous god. *You shall have no other gods before me.* Yet the crucifixes that hang on walls all over Rome are no different than Nebuchadnezzar's statue.

The curate leans back against the cushions on his chair; his plump hands pat his knees. She has decided to call him Curate *Cachèmme*, a windbag who manages to make the shortest story long.

"So, my beloved child, it will be for you as it was for Hananiah, Misa, and Azariah. In this place, and in our hands, you, too, will be saved from the flames. Do you understand the meaning of this story?"

Of course, she understands the story, but does he?

"You, too, have been thrown into the fiery pit," he says, licking his lips and folding his plump hands across his round belly, "but yours are flames of purification from which you will emerge redeemed, recognizing the truth of the Catholic faith. Your soul will be saved, and you will delight in the grace of God. In his Epistle to the Romans, Saint Paul wrote that all Israel shall be saved, and his prophecy is coming true, beloved daughter, one conversion at a time."

She raises her gaze to meet brown eyes buried in puffy cheeks. He smiles expectantly, as though his story has worked a miracle conversion. "Thank you," she says, "but I have no need of your prayers, which only serve to tie me to this place. And I cannot agree with your interpretation of the Book of Daniel. In the Book of Exodus, it is written that God said, 'You shall not make for yourself a carved image, or any likeness of anything that is in heaven above or that is in the earth beneath or that is in the water under the earth.' Yet you pray to likenesses of your saints, your mother of God, your Jesus Christ. You choose to impose your own meaning on the text because it supports your arguments. My belief is different, and your distortions of the Torah will never persuade me to believe as you do."

She sees in his face that he considers himself an authority on religion and considers her a little Jewess who amounts to nothing.

He stands up, his fists clenched at his sides, and says, "You are an impudent and stubborn girl. Why is it so difficult for you to accept the wisdom of a man who is much older and more learned than yourself?"

"I am very sorry, sir, but I have not been taught to accept. I have been taught to ponder, to question, to think. I do not need to pray to your pictures or your statues. God is with me everywhere, and I pray directly to him. Now I have said too much, and I ask your forgiveness, but I have said nothing that I do not know to be true. I did not ask for your prayers, Signor Curate. I ask only that you allow me to return to my parents."

He turns and pounds the door, which is instantly unlocked. She thinks the prioress must have been waiting there in hope of hearing the glad news of her conversion.

The door closes behind him, and Anna hovers, listening, silently laughing as Curate Cachèmme whispers with the prioress, sighing in exasperation at the stubborn little Jewess. And then the key turns in the lock and she remembers that she is a prisoner.

~

AN UNMARRIED woman is never alone in the company of a man. At home, Anna would not even put her face to the window, but here she is deprived of her modesty. They come in twos or threes, monks, preachers, priests. Night and day, they invade her cell, and she has not a moment's privacy. She has no idea what their ranks are or what their costumes mean, although she can guess how important each of them considers himself by measuring his arrogance. Often the prioress stays in the cell during these lectures, and when they finish, she sends in young nuns who never speak to her at all.

Every night of her life, Anna slept under the same roof, surrounded by her family. Now she sees only strangers, enemies who want to steal her soul. Every day of her life, she did the same chores, said the same prayers, read the same books. Now she longs for a few lines of Horace, Cicero, or Ovid. If only she had a bit of fabric to embroider, a hem to roll, something useful to do with her hands!

Every woman in the ghetto can sew, embroider, turn a buttonhole. Handiwork is no guarantee against abject poverty, but it is the most effective insurance available. Even the brightest girls are not permitted to study at the Talmùd Torà school with the boys, and certainly not at the advanced Accademia-Jeshiva. But from the moment they begin to talk, Jewish mothers teach their daughters to read. Anna toddled up and down the Strada della Rua holding her mother's hand, reading signs in front of the shops, the price lists, the flyers affixed to the walls. Books filled her home, stacked on tables, on floors. Books in Hebrew, Italian, Latin. Old books with cracked leather covers and a musty smell. Her father said that if a man spends money on a good bottle of wine, he drinks it and then it is gone. But if he spends money on a good book, he can read it again and again for the rest of his life.

Anna can read and write beautifully in Italian, respectably in Hebrew, passably well in Latin. She long ago memorized all the prayers a Jewish woman should know and the melodies that go with them. She can set a sabbath table, pray over the lighting of the candles. She could even kosher a chicken if she had to, but she will never be called upon to do it. Her family can afford to pay the butcher for that, and whichever man she marries will surely provide her with the same small comforts her father has given her. But she would know if a chicken had not been koshered properly and would complain of it.

Every week, the dance master came to their rooms to instruct her and her sister. They learned the minuet, the *contredance* and the *folies d'Espagne*. A music master came to teach Anna to play the *tiorba* and Allegrezza the mandolin.

Their father believes in educating his daughters, though not in the same way that he educated his son. Tranquillo was a student of the great Rabbi Corcos, who insisted that a Jew needs to know more than the Torah. He taught Tranquillo philosophy, history, and the Latin poets, and Tranquillo taught them to Anna.

Jews are excluded from every guild, permitted only to trade in used things, old things. The del Monte family trades in very old things, antiques. Newly wealthy Christian bankers, freshly titled noblemen, bishops, and cardinals buy up Rome's derelict palaces. Baruch del Monte furnishes their abandoned rooms with velvet draperies, statuary, paintings, Venetian chandeliers, Persian carpets, French porcelain, English crystal, inlaid dining tables, and enough matching chairs to seat a party of forty. His clients claim that all these things are their own family heirlooms—even the ancestral portraits. And Baruch del Monte will never say otherwise.

He believes that a Jewish woman will not survive this world without certain manly skills. He says that a Jewish wife should be able to help her husband in his business, as his wife Belfiore and his mother Savta Rachele have done. And if a woman finds herself a widow, she should be able to run the business herself, to bargain, negotiate, sign contracts. She should be able to support herself and her children, to defend herself if need be. He tells his children that a man needs more than a willing body in his bed and a womb to bear his descendants. Mammà pretends to be horrified when he says these things, but Anna knows she is secretly laughing.

Mammà says a man needs a partner with a good mind to help him sort out his thoughts, to filter his ideas. She says that men have a lot of responsibility, and that they are always secretly afraid. A man needs a wife to tell him he is not a failure when he is doing badly and to tell him he is not a god when he is doing well. Ovid said, "*Si qua voles apte nubere, nube pari.*" If you wish to marry well, marry an equal. Baruch del Monte says, "A smart woman makes a good wife."

～

No Jew has enough space for privacy at home. The scòla is filled with curious idlers who make it their clubhouse, and if they were to meet there, it would expose their Catholic lawyer to the risk of being denounced by the Church. So, the men have crowded onto the benches in the windowless back room of Elio Terracini's inn and ordered a liter of wine. A burning strip of cloth in a saucer full of tallow grease provides the only light.

How many times have the memunim, governors of the ghetto, fought to retrieve a Jew from the Catacumeni? They rarely succeed, but from each failure they extract a clue, a bit of information, and they use it to construe a new strategy. They have discovered the cause of Anna del Monte's abduction. Their plan is to secure her release by giving Vicegerent de' Rossi the arguments he needs to persuade the pope, who relishes discussing the fine points of his own decrees.

The three memunim have assumed the detached calm of businessmen at a negotiation, which enrages Baruch del Monte, who has not been calm for an instant since his daughter was abducted. The lawyer, Gaspare Battaglia, bewigged and dressed like a cleric in a black abitocorto and white lace, keeps his hands busy, unrolling the petition on the table, finding spaces between the jug and the cups. "I believe that our difficulties are not with de' Rossi," he says, finally resting his hands in his lap. "The vicegerent ordered Anna's abduction only because he was compelled to do so. It is the Rector of the Casa dei Catacumeni, Mileti, who insists on keeping her indefinitely. To be sure, de' Rossi would like to overrule him. The pope will oppose it, but I believe we can help de' Rossi to find a way around that."

The lawyer's sympathies are with these Jews. The del Monte family hired him when he was a young lawyer without clients, and they have treated him fairly and honestly through three generations. Although he would never dare to voice his opinion, the tenets of Christianity, as he understands them, do not include tearing children and young women from their families.

He says, "I believe that Anna's continued detention would not reflect well on the vicegerent. Even if she is held at the Casa dei Catacumeni for the full quarantine, her case would eventually be overturned by the Tribunal of the Inquisition—assuming she does not relent."

Angelo Zevi, bald and bearded, has a laugh that reminds the lawyer of a goose. Now he makes the noise geese make when they rush towards their feed, snorting through his nose. "My niece is the most committed Jew in the ghetto. It would be easier to convert Rabbi Mielì!"

Baruch del Monte's eyes never leave the table. "I am sorry, but I cannot laugh, Angelo. I am a man struggling to untie his own hands. De' Rossi opposes forced conversions, but who is to say what is forced? If you confine a young woman for weeks and months, tempt her, threaten her, tell her that she will never see her family again, and eventually she surrenders, has she been converted of her own free will?"

The lawyer ignores him. He is intent on delivering the petition to the vicegerent in the morning. He dips a quill in ink and hands it to Angelo Zevi. "Would you like to be the first to sign?" And so, it is done, three signatures, the ink powdered dry, the document rolled and fastened with the seal of the Hebrew Community of Rome. The lawyer pulls the lace cuffs of his sleeves down and begins to replace the documents in his leather bag. He is a busy man who earns only a small fee for each case, and so is forced to hurry from one client to the next. "I will leave you now," he says. "I think we have written a good petition. De' Rossi's power is great but not without limit. He knows that endlessly detaining the obstinate daughter of a prominent Jewish family will only make his life more difficult. I am sorry, Baruch. I know how it is for you."

"You know, Gaspare? How can you know? Who is going to steal your children away from you? Who? Forgive me. You have been a friend to us, how many years? You danced at my wedding and at my son's wedding. But I swear to you, I will stop at nothing to save my Channà. If the whole of the ghetto rises up and makes war, so be it."

Moisé Modigliano reaches for the wine. "Come, Baruch. We should drink a little. I am not sleeping well, myself. I warn my daughters to be careful what they say. You never know who is listening. This is not a way to live, always in fear. Little children are abducted while they innocently play in the street. I would never allow a goi to enter my home, not even a *scékez* to light the fire on the sabbath, for fear she might get it into her head to douse our children with water and call them baptized."

Baruch del Monte stands up, buttons his frock coat. His brother-in-law, Angelo Zevi, follows him out. The main room of the inn is choked with smoke and redolent with the meaty odor of smoldering tallow. The two men move quickly, nodding at neighbors, avoiding conversation. They merge into the glow of a sunset that gilds even the dimmest streets of Rome. A breeze lifts bits of trash from the cobblestones and tosses them about.

Angelo speaks very quietly. "Baruch, I need to tell you something. Belfiore came to the store yesterday to see me. Did you know? She has the greatest faith in you. Please, don't misunderstand, but I am her older brother.

We have been orphaned for many years, so she has always expected me to defend the family."

Baruch pulls on his beard. "She came to see you? Already, I think she wants to divorce me. She watched me do nothing while they took our Channà away. That *gonif bargello* should have shot me. It would have been better. When Belfiore thinks I am not looking, she sits and stares, half dead. If I touch her shoulder, she smiles, but she is not herself. Allegrezza stays beside her mother from morning till night. Is this a way for a young woman about to be married?"

His lament is interrupted by shouts, the pounding of boots on cobblestones. Tranquillo del Monte and Gabriele Sereni cross the little Piazzetta del Pancotto and rush towards them. "*Aùh!*" Baruch points with his chin. "You see how fine they look, a pair of *demonà*, young and energetic, straight and tall, capes slung over their shoulders. They resemble you and I, Angelo, when we were young. Now you are forty-six years of age, and I am an old man of forty-nine, stumbling over my feet, consumed by fury and fear."

Tranquillo, breathless from hurrying, kisses his father and uncle on both cheeks. "Tatà, we were coming to meet you."

"What's all this running? You missed nothing, 'quillo. Go home to your wife."

"*Badonai*, Tatà! Why can I never talk to you seriously? What did Gnóro Battaglia say? I tell you that when de' Rossi finds no benefit for himself in keeping her, Channà will be released. Can we persuade him of that? Will the petition be delivered in the morning? May I read it?"

His father stares straight ahead, the tip of his tongue hooked in the corner of his mouth.

"Tatà? How are you?"

"How should I be? Go home. You too, Angelo, go with Tranquillo and Gabriele. I want to walk a little by myself. Besides, how far is it that I need company?"

FOR A few minutes, the three men walk silently along the Vicolo delle Azzimelle, then Gabriele leaves them, cutting through an alley so narrow a man with outstretched arms can touch the walls on both sides. Tranquillo watches his friend disappear into the shadows before he speaks. Some things he shares only with family.

"*Senti, zio,*" he says softly. "I know you sent gifts to de' Rossi and to the Cardinal. I was standing in the doorway of the shop when the boy came with his cart. He fetched two heavy bundles with their names written in big letters. What have you sent? Silks? Brocades? Did you include a 'most humble' entreaty? You prefer not to answer me?"

Angelo inhales a goosey laugh. "You are very confident, *fijemo*. But you have not seen what I have seen."

It is often like this with Dod Angelo, who chooses to laugh at his nephew when a few words of encouragement are needed. Now he says, "You must never trust the goim to follow their own rules, not where Jews are concerned."

Tranquillo stops walking, prepares himself for the instruction he knows will come, faking a solemn nod from time to time, as though every word were a revelation.

"You must never assume that anyone, Christian or Jew, will honor a bargain or make good on a bribe. Learn that now, and never forget it. Some popes are worse than others. The one who graces us now will not rest until every Jew in the ghetto is counting rosary beads, but we must never forget to hope that this time will be different, that this time we will be treated fairly. Now, come, my Ester waits for you every night."

TRANQUILLO DEL Monte has been in love with his *bat-doda*, his cousin Ester, for as long as he can remember, but he could not marry her until he was twenty-four years old. It is not so uncommon in the crowded ghetto for young people to wait to marry until they can find a room of their own. Poor couples have to wait for a death in the family. Tranquillo and Ester were more fortunate, but still they waited for Ester's brother to marry and move in with his wife's family. They are newlyweds, but it is as if they have always been married and always will be.

When Ester was a three-year old toddler with copper curls flowing down her back, seven-year-old Tranquillo kissed her cheek. She put her finger in her mouth and laughed and he thought he would faint from happiness. When she was seven years old, and he was eleven, he held her hand as they ran through the streets of the ghetto, shrieking with laughter. When he was thirteen, he became a man, but he dared only squeeze Ester's hand and kiss her hair, and only if he thought no one was looking.

Everyone in the family assumed they would marry. Even after Ester began her monthly bleeding, they let them be, so long as they were not alone. Tranquillo has never looked at another woman. His cousin is everything a man could want in a wife—an excellent cook, an enthusiastic lover, and an intelligent woman with whom he can have a good discussion. But she is not like his sister.

Channà devours anything with words on it. It worries him that no man will be a good match for such a woman. Gabriele Sereni looks at her and she looks back. He is a nice enough fellow, a good friend, but how well can he discuss Cicero and Ovid?

As the sunset glow fades into a melancholy dusk, Baruch del Monte walks slowly along the Via della Scòla Catalana, head down, hands clasped behind his back. Shopkeepers are closing up, dragging heavy baskets inside. He avoids greeting them, fearful of seeing the depths of his grief reflected in their eyes. Everyone in the ghetto knows what happened to his Channà.

A lamp is lit in this window, then that one. He can smell a beef bone simmering in a pot somewhere, onions frying in goose fat. He is at home here. Tonight, he will sleep in the former palace of the Boccapaduli, where his family has slept for nearly two hundred years. His wife, his mother, his daughter Allegrezza are waiting for him there in large rooms with high ceilings, now shabby, once grand.

The marble staircase that leads from the ground floor to the *piano nobile* has not been repaired in decades. The steps are cracked and treacherous, but he takes them two at a time. He opens the door to their rooms and enters calling, "Belfiore! Dodi! I have news! Gaspare is confident that de' Rossi will release Channà. We have written an excellent appeal. Our arguments are indisputable!"

Belfiore covers her face with her hands, hiding her doubts. She knows that her husband does not believe his own words, but hope is a game they play. "*Speriamo*," she says. "Let us hope." Allegrezza looks up from the table where she has been peeling potatoes and stares at her mother, looking for a reaction. All day, they talk of nothing but Channà. "Go next door, *fijema*," her mother says, "Go tell Savta Rachele."

Most Illustrious Archbishop of Tarso, Vicegerent of the city

THE PUBLIC REPRESENTATIVES
OF THE HEBREW COMMUNITY OF ROME,
with hearts full of gratitude for your past indulgences, and fully aware of the generosity with which you have always treated the Jews of Rome, most humbly beseech you to consider

Sabato Coen, an unmarried man enamored of the Hebrew spinster Anna del Monte, daughter of Benedetto del Monte and his wife, Belfiore Zevi, having been unsuccessful in his attempt to make Anna his wife and embittered by the repugnance shown by her parents, has converted to the Christian faith and, in the presence of the notary of the cardinal vicar and the vicegerent, and witnessed by two other recent converts, has falsely sworn that he was betrothed to the aforementioned young woman. As a result of this false claim, Anna del Monte has been wrongfully abducted from the home of her parents and is being kept at the Casa dei Catacumeni.

In his Extreme Goodness, His Holiness Benedetto XIV has thoroughly studied our Jewish Laws and Customs regarding engagements and marriages and has declared that a bride-to-be can be taken to the Casa dei Catacumeni so long as there is a reasonable conjecture of betrothal, even if the engagement has not been carried out according to Jewish ritual, which requires a notarized agreement signed by both sets of parents. As there was no betrothal agreement of any kind, not even according to the more lenient customs of a Catholic engagement, and as both parents of Anna del Monte, her brother Tranquillo del Monte, the Rabbi Mielì, all three public representatives of the ghetto, as well as twenty-four neighbors living in the same building or buildings adjacent to that occupied by the del Monte family have issued sworn statements that no such betrothal can be reasonably construed, there can be no basis whatsoever to support the claim sworn by Sabato Coen.

The continued forced detention of Anna del Monte can only serve to foment greater hatred of the Catholic Church on the part of the Jews who already view every conversion as an act of violence against them. Such abductions risk producing insincere declarations of conversion, which are likely to result in apostasy.

Moreover, the abduction of Anna del Monte defies the just sentiments of the Sacred Office, which, in its great wisdom, has realized that such unwarranted abduction only threatens the fragile stability of the Roman Jewish community and threatens to unhinge relations between the ghetto and the Catholic authorities. Often Converts and Neophytes denounce or even offer young women whom they desire to marry when they have been refused. From this it ensues that a Jewish father can no longer be sure of his own daughters at home, and the women of the ghetto have been continually subjected to false depositions.

The difficulties of a Jew becoming a good and useful Christian are reflected in the care with which the sincerity of intention has always been scrutinized, even in cases of purely voluntarily admission into the Casa dei Catacumeni.

Therefore, with the greatest respect and humility, we beseech your most esteemed Excellency to release Anna del Monte and to allow her to return to her parents.

Angelo Zevi   Samuele Corcos
Moisé Modigliano

Governors of the Hebrew Community of Rome

S HE SLEEPS little in this place, where they wake her in the night to torment her with their endless preaching. And when, at last, she is able to sleep, she does not sleep well. She suspects they have given her this horrid straw mattress so that she will be too exhausted to resist their endless preaching.

She does not trust the food here, which surely does not adhere to the *kasher* laws she follows at home. She has asked the prioress to send her a boiled egg every evening so that each day she can hide a bit of eggshell at the back of the food box. This morning she adds another bit, marking the third day of her imprisonment. In this way, she will count the days, so that no matter what they do to confuse her, she will always know how long she has been here.

A Jew who has been accused of wishing to convert can be kept for only twelve days. If she never says the word "yes," if she admits to nothing, in nine more days they will have to release her. In nine more days, she will be back with her family in the *miqudash m'at*, the little haven, the ghetto.

But what if "yes" is the truth? Will the God of Abraham forgive a lie? The Holy One, blessed be He, despises a person who says one thing with his mouth and hides another in his heart. There are exceptions. If the bride is ugly, it is permissible to say she is lovely. If a man has an incurable illness, it is permissible to comfort him by saying the doctors are hopeful. What trick question will these priests ask her to which the only true answer is "yes?" Will she be tempted to lie to save herself? If she lies instead to save her family from grief, will her god forgive her? She has never knowingly told a lie in her life, but she has never been away from her family, locked in a Catholic cell.

When the prioress comes to the cell, she squeezes Anna's hands, strokes her cheek, and tells her that she prays for her soul. Anna thinks the old nun truly believes that she will spend eternity in hell if she refuses to convert and means to save her from infernal anguish. She has been given fresh underthings and her embroidered cotton shift has been replaced with a rough linen one. She feels cleaner, but she dreams of the ghetto bathhouse, of scrubbing herself under the steam.

It has been ten days since she went to the *mikveh* bath to purify herself after bleeding, ten days since she inserted a scrap of white linen between her legs, making sure it was unstained when she pulled it out. In a few days, she will begin to bleed again. Will the nuns provide her with bits of cotton to absorb the blood? How will she keep herself clean?

~

THIS MORNING, the prioress impressed upon her that she was to be greatly honored by the visit of an archbishop, a man of very high rank. As the fat Curate *Cachèmme* failed to convert her with his bible story, she is to be persuaded by the efforts of a more exalted cleric.

Indeed, he is dressed in a princely stole, his arms incased in wide bands of white lace and the cross that hangs on a heavy gold chain over his breast is encrusted with emeralds. But he walks as though he were holding something between his buttocks and is terrified that it will slip out. He lowers himself onto the chair with great care, and as he has not demanded extra cushions, she hopes that he will not stay with her very long.

"My daughter, I am the Archbishop of San Celso," he says. He speaks the elegant Italian of a nobleman, but Anna is astonished by the timbre of his voice, which is high and pinched, like the voice of the woman who sells buttons on the Vicolo della Torre. He leans forward as though he might spring up at any moment. "I have a tale for you this morning," he says, and she hopes that it will be less boring than the story the Curate Cachèmme told her the day before.

"God said to Abraham," he begins, "go from your land, from your birthplace and from the house of your father. Go to the land that I will show you."

Every six-year-old yeshivot boy knows this story. The

Lech Lechà. She knows the man will make his point eventually, but he will have to distort the text to do it. The religion of Abraham is the true religion. It is the religion of her father and mother, her grandparents, and all those who lived before them. The Archbishop keeps talking. He has made an endless *meghillà* from a few lines of the Torah, adding his own specious commentary.

To hear this ancient biblical tale recounted in the voice of a button seller is so funny she is afraid she will insult him by laughing. He gestures with his fingers gracefully splayed, his chin lifted as though he is forever sniffing the air. Anna covers her face with her hands to hide her expression. She does not wish to appear disrespectful to so exalted a person, but she is too tired, too frightened to restrain her laughter for long.

She rubs her eyes, then lowers her hands with a great show of forcing her eyes to open. If the great archbishop notices her rudeness, he says nothing. She distracts herself by watching his rosy lips, the tight smile that flashes whenever he pauses. She sees that he is not a young man, but his skin is still soft and unblemished, his features almost girlish. She thinks he is too proud of his thick hair to wear a wig, and his bright beretta floats prettily over his graying curls.

"Dear daughter," he says. His voice rises and falls like a popular melody. "If you wish to acquire the grace of God, you must do as Abraham has done. You must leave behind your goods, your father, your mother, and all the things of this world in order to embrace the true God and save your soul."

Ah, so that is the point of the story. He thinks he can persuade her to willingly abandon her life.

"I pity you very much," he says, leaning his face towards her, "for you will be sorry to lose your home and your family, but all that you will lose is as nothing compared to what you will gain in the true faith. On the contrary, you will find a hundred times more than you leave behind. And in the next life, you will be sure to live in paradise among the angels. When you embrace Christianity, you will no longer witness the misery of your people, who are continuously burdened with hardships, abandoned by God and their fellow men, without priests, without altars and without sacrifices, scattered to the four corners of the world, slaves, subjects of every ruler, lower even than the rabble. If your religion were as true as you believe it to be, you would be honored and respected by all nations as you were when you were still under the grace of God, when you were in Jerusalem before the coming of the Messiah in whom you refuse to believe."

The Archbishop has made a drama of this last bit, turning his mouth down like the mask of tragedy, dabbing at his eyes with his lace handkerchief. She thinks he is right to say that the Jews have been continuously burdened with hardships. Roman Jews are the unwelcome guests of a host who changes every few years. A new pope could decide to banish them at any time for any reason. The families who attend the Scòla Siciliano, the Scòla Catalina and the Scòla Castigliano were driven from Spain and Portugal, from Naples and Sicily.

At least once a year, something frightens her father into believing that the pope will expel them. He sits at the head of the table and reminds his family that Jews have been in Rome for nearly two thousand years. Allegrezza and Anna lower their heads so that he will not see them rolling their eyes. Tatà says that they have remained Jewish through the destruction of Jerusalem by Titus, the destruction of Rome by the barbarians, through the penalties and punishments of emperor after emperor, pope after pope. And she stares at her plate, hoping that he will finish his speech soon and say the prayer, so that she can wash the dishes and get back to the book she has been reading.

Now she is locked in a convent with an archbishop who thinks that by telling her a story she already knows very well, he will persuade her to forsake the faith of her ancestors.

She has neither been asked nor answered a single question, yet the archbishop seems quite satisfied that his visit has been successful. He draws a cross in the air, his hand so heavy with rings she is amazed that he can lift it. In the high-pitched voice of the button seller he says, "I pray with tears in my eyes that God may enlighten you and that you will not be obstinate. For were it not for the mercy of God and of the reigning princes, and the communion of saints, your people would not survive. I implore you to consider what I have said, and with that I leave you with my blessings."

IN THE narrow Vicolo della Torre, the button-seller squats from morning to evening, her wares displayed on the pavement in front of her. She has arranged them artfully on the best scrap of cloth she can find, and tidies them relentlessly, moving a button half a centimeter closer to another, half a centimeter farther away. If she sees a clean pair of shoes headed in her direction, she lifts her head and calls out in a high-pitched voice, "*Bottoni, pizzi, fiocchi!*" Buttons, lace, bows.

At dusk, she sits with her two daughters on the stoop of the building where they sleep and eat, using a tiny knife to remove buttons, laces and other refinements from old garments too worn to be repaired. The next morning, her husband will add the stripped-down rags to the bundle he carries each day to the market at Piazza Navona to sell. And if he has a good day, they will have a bit of goose fat to spread on their bread that night.

When they can afford it, they buy bread. And when they cannot, they wait for the weekly visit of the *Gemìlut Chasadim*, the charitable society. The more fortunate ghetto families of the Strada della Rua and the Piazza del Scòle venture down to the Strada della Fiumara in their oldest shoes, their skirts tied up to avoid the dust and excrement. The Zevi, the Modigliano, the Corcos, the Ambròn and the del Monte bring medicine, bedclothes, bread, meat and prayers. It is the duty of every Jew to show loving kindness to his impoverished neighbors. And if he should fail in his duty, the temple will punish him with a fine.

ON THE High Holy Days, before Baruch del Monte enters the sanctuary of the scòla, he takes a moment to shake hands with the *gabbai* who care for the temple, the officials and the idle gossips who mill about the back of the room, allowing them to admire his coat, the quality of the fabric, the knife-sharp fit of the shoulders. He may wear the cast-off clothing of a wealthy gentile, but his mother, his wife, and his daughters are all expert tailors who can invisibly repair a tear, remake, and refit any garment. The precisely folded prayer shawl, which he carries under his arm, belonged to his grandfather. Blue stripes are woven into the wide length of white silk and the del Monte family crest—three mountain peaks topped by a crescent moon—is embroidered at both ends. When he unfurls the shawl and wraps it around his shoulders, it extends below his knees.

But this morning, as he prepares to walk through the Porta di Giudea, Baruch del Monte feels neither pleasure nor pride. The fabric of his coat is fine, the fit impeccable, but as the sumptuary laws dictate that no Jew shall appear outside the ghetto in clothing unbefitting his station, his garments are dun-colored, without a trace of embellishment.

Money lending made generations of del Montes wealthy, but in 1682, a papal bull rescinded the Jews' banking licenses. Rich Jewish bankers had supported the entire ghetto for more than a century. When they could no longer provide large sums, all Jews were doomed to one form of poverty or another. The new law was nearly as calamitous for wealthy Catholics, whose lavish lifestyles had been financed by Jewish credit. The Roman economy nearly collapsed.

On the morning in 1749 when Baruch del Monte examines himself in the mirror, Jewish banking has been banned for three generations. But a nobleman with a gambling debt or a high-ranking cleric who has borrowed unwisely from the Vatican can still call upon a Jew, so long as it is the right Jew, to resolve his dilemma. Baruch can be trusted to behave with a delicacy and discretion Catholics consider rare among his breed. If he is offered a painting, a blown-glass vase, an elaborately carved and inlaid desk, or a set of silver chalices, it is understood that he will never disclose from whom he bought them, and that the price he pays will be only slightly less than the items are worth. A messenger appears at a side door. Money passes from gloved hand to gloved hand. Later, when the precious heirloom is in danger of being missed, del Monte can be trusted to sell it back to its previous owner for a price only moderately higher than the sum he paid for it. Money changes hands again, and it is as if neither transaction ever occurred.

The impoverished duke who saved face by providing his daughter with a respectable dowry would not like it known that the money came from a Jew. Baruch del Monte would never betray the confidence of this man. He would never blackmail the duke or humiliate the daughter. But his own daughter, his Channà, is imprisoned in a convent, and the secrets of rich and powerful gentiles are the only weapons he has. The Sant' Uffizio, the tribunal of the Inquisition, meets on Wednesdays at the Piazza Minerva, and one of the twelve cardinals who sits in judgement is the duke's brother.

Belfiore stands behind her husband, pulling on the hem of his frock coat, adjusting the shoulders. Her eyes inspect every inch in search of a stray thread, a bit of lint. Baruch grimaces at his reflection then turns to embrace his wife. They have prepared small velvet pouches with coins for the duke's doorkeeper and his footman, and for the duke himself, the gift of a diamond cravat pin that has lately come into Baruch's possession. Belfiore places the pouches in her husband's leather shoulder bag, then hands him the hat he so despises. Even he, a del Monte, nominated for life to the ruling Council of Sixty, a man known for his knowledge and wisdom, his fear of God and his opposition to evil, even he must identify himself as Jewish. No matter how carefully he dresses, outside the ghetto gates, he is no more than a Jew in a drab suit and a yellow tricorn hat.

THE BELL sounds as though it is inside her head, not somewhere above it. The prioress has told her that the bell calls the nuns to evening prayers, although it can hardly inspire contemplation. She has brought a lamp with enough oil to last two hours and has told Anna that she, too, must use this time for reflection. Still, her mind races like a mouse chased by a broom, desperately searching for refuge where there is none to be found.

Weeks ago, her grandmother gave her an amulet. She called it a *chimiangk* and pressed it into Anna's hand as though it were a thing of great value. It is nothing more than a bit of parchment inscribed with cryptic symbols and the Hebrew initials A G L A, *Ateh Gibur Leo Adonai*, the Lord ever powerful. She folded it, placed it in a silk pouch threaded with ribbon, and told Anna to wear it around her neck to protect her spirit.

Belfiore del Monte thinks her mother-in-law's Cabalistic beliefs are nonsense. She would have nothing kind to say if she saw the amulet, so Anna hid it in the pocket of her skirt. She can hardly imagine what these priests and nuns would do if they discovered it. She knows that a bit of parchment can never protect her, but it comforts her to feel the little silk square with her fingers, to think of Savta's wrinkled face, her dry lips pressed against Anna's forehead.

Overwrought Catholic women come to the ghetto every day to buy potions and amulets from old women who sit in the shadows with their secrets. Housewives come to buy cheap used goods. Merchants come to arrange illegal loans in Jacob the Jeweler's back room. Priests and nuns, monks and friars come to have a cape mended or a shoe repaired, their eyes darting about in fear and wonder. But when night falls, all the goim are gone, the ghetto gates are locked, and Anna is safe.

When she was very small, her world was wholly Jewish. She was a curious girl, but she was not at all interested in life outside the ghetto. Her family, her friends, the bed she shared with her sister, the songs they sang, the foods they ate, the games they played, everything that mattered was enclosed in walls whose gates were locked one hour after dusk and opened one hour after dawn.

Anna was six years old when she left the ghetto for the first time. That morning she sat with her sister on the edge of their parents' bed, impatiently swinging her legs, watching Mammà pin a yellow scarf to her thick auburn hair. Mammà often told Anna that although curiosity was good, asking too many questions was not good. It was impolite, annoying. She told her to choose her questions carefully and to ask only one or two.

"Mammà, why are you wearing that scarf? Why don't you wear your pretty hat with the red feathers?"

"Because, Channà, outside the ghetto I wear the *sciamanno*."

"Why, Mammà?"

"So that everyone will know we are Jews."

"Why, Mammà?"

"So that the goim will not come near us."

"Why, Mammà?"

"No more 'why, why,' Channà! There is no 'why.'"

They walked down the wide, broken staircase, watching every step, afraid of loosening a piece of cracked marble, then across the market square and out the gate, into the Piazza Giudea, into another world.

"What is that house, Mammà?"

"That is the guardhouse where the pope's sbirri keep watch to be sure we follow all their rules."

"What rules, Mammà?"

"No more questions, Channà. Your brother will tell you later. Ask Tranquillo."

"Who lives over there, Mammà, in those streets?"

"Ask me something else…. No, listen to me, I will tell you. In those houses, thirty rods from the ghetto, live the *neofiti*, Jews who have become goim. We are forbidden to go to their houses, and they are forbidden to come to ours or even to speak with us."

"Why, Mammà?"

"Because they have traded their souls for money. The Catholic Church pays one hundred *scudi* to a Jew who becomes a Catholic. The pope is afraid that if a convert should even look at a Jew, his heart would break, and he would return to us."

"Why? What would happen if they came home to the ghetto?"

"*Aùh*! Channà! Nothing good would happen. Ask your brother."

They passed a building with an enormous clock at the top and a door as tall as three men standing on each other's shoulders. Anna had never seen such a building. She was afraid to ask Mammà any more questions, so she whispered to her sister.

"That? They call it a church. The goim pray there."

"Why is it so big?"

"Because there are so many goim."

"How many goim could there possibly be to need such an enormous place for praying?"

A carriage rolled by, drawn by four horses. Two men stood on the back, holding on for their lives, dressed in such finery, Anna wondered why they were not permitted to ride inside. She had never seen such a thing. The ghetto streets are much too narrow for such a carriage, and, in any case, Jews are not allowed to own carriages. If a horse comes into the ghetto, he is delivering a nobleman or dragging a cart.

Mammà pulled her daughters out of the street and pressed them against the building with her arm. As the carriage passed, dust rose around them, and Anna covered her face with her hands, but she peeked between her fingers. "Another church?" she whispered to Allegrezza.

"The goim have a million enormous churches. Ask Tranquillo why. He knows."

"The whole ghetto could fit into that church!"

The street was lined with shops—like the Strada della Rua in the ghetto but wider, brighter. Fabrics hung from low roofs that shaded the entryways. Women stood on the thresholds, crossed arms squashing their big breasts. They called out to the passersby in the street. "What are you looking for? Linen? Cotton? I have it here." Men milled about in bunches, talking and smoking pipes.

Mammà was going to visit a man who had something for Tatà. She said, "Why should he take a chance if he doesn't have to? No one will bother a Jewish housewife with two little girls." She said that the pope's law forbids Jews to do business with goim, although goim do business with Jews all the time.

The street emptied out into a piazza so big the horses waiting at the far end looked like toys. "Campo de' Fiori," Mammà said. Sometimes she knew Anna was about to ask a question before she even opened her mouth. "It used to be a field of flowers. I think so. Stay close to me. Hold on to your sister."

Near the middle of the piazza was a pole so tall Anna had to lean her head all the way back to see the top. Allegrezza whispered, "The goim use that pole to torture people who break their rules. They hang men by their arms with ropes, then they pull them up to the top and drop them to the ground so their shoulders break. Tranquillo told me."

Anna asked no more questions.

W HEN SHE awoke, Anna could smell rain.
She could hear it crashing onto the street
below. She has been locked up for only
four days, but already it amazes her that there is still a
sky outside, that there is still such a thing as weather. She
pulls the wooden chair up to the window so that she can
stand on it and presses her face against the bars, breathing in the damp air, watching the brick wall change colors as it gets wet. There are four bits of eggshell in the
back of the food box. In eight more days, they will have
to release her.

ANNA DEL Monte is in the kitchen, talking to her sister, stirring the polenta, pretending that she isn't waiting,
that her ears aren't tuned to the sound of her brother's

boots on the stairs, the sound of his books dropping on the sitting room floor.

Two books make a dull noise; three books make a soft thud, but this afternoon the books crash onto the floor. At least four. He has new books! What books? Mammà silently picks up the wooden spoon her daughter has abandoned and continues the stirring.

The top of Anna's head barely reaches her brother's chest. Her arms are too short to close around his waist. He is tall, big enough to protect her, playful enough to torment her. She thinks she had better hug him right away to be sure he will be generous with her later.

She feels his belly vibrate under her cheek, his laughter fizzle over her. "Horace," he says. "Rabbi Corcos lent me a book of Horace this afternoon."

"I didn't ask you anything, Tranquillo."

"But you wanted to ask."

She is already kneeling over the books. "Is it this one?"

"Shouldn't you be helping Mammà?"

"I helped her already. Allegrezza is helping now."

He calls out to the kitchen. "Mammà?"

"Let her read, 'quillo. Your father wants her to read."

And they read. Before the meal, after the meal. Sitting on the carpet, on the floor, at the table in the kitchen, on the cracked marble steps that lead to the front door. Tranquillo spends his days studying at the *beth midras* of the synagogue. Anna spends her days at home with her mother, her grandmother, her sister. She cooks, she sews, she cleans. And then she reads.

Tranquillo and Anna read Horace until their father locks up the store and comes home. After the meal, after the women have cleaned the kitchen, the family is gathered in the sitting room, Mammà and Allegrezza with their sewing, Tatà with his pipe, Tranquillo and Anna with the first book of odes by Quintus Horatius Flaccus.

"'*Iam satis terris nivis atque dire grandinis misit Pater et rubente.* The father sent snow and dreaded hail to earth, striking sacred hills with a fiery hand to frighten the city.' Have I translated correctly, Tranquillo?"

Allegrezza looks up as though her sister's voice has interfered with her sewing. "Channà! Read silently. Read to yourself!"

"Let Channà read, Alle. Go on, read, *fijama.* Tatà is listening."

Belfiore has heard her husband say this too many times. "*Ahi,* Baruch! Isn't it enough she knows all the psalms in Hebrew? Does she also have to know Latin, the language of the goim?

"Every night, you say the same thing, Belfiore. Let her read."

Anna is waiting, a finger pressed against the next line of the poem. "Tranquillo, if I come across a new word, can I ask you the meaning?"

"If I say 'yes,' or if I say 'no,' you will ask. So, ask."

A	S THE bells announced midday with twelve deafening peals, the nun in the black veil unlocked the door to Anna's cell and the three who had been kneeling by her bed all morning tucked their rosaries into the pockets of their habits and flew off like pigeons from a tree, robes fluttering behind them.

Now she is alone for a few blessed moments. How is such silence possible in a place inhabited by many women? How do the priests, bishops, and archbishops glide so noiselessly in and out? Why are there no sounds of weeping, no cries from the other cells? Is she the only woman who laments her imprisonment? What has happened to the little children, the Jewish babies who are offered to the Church, torn from the arms of their anguished mothers and brought to this place to be baptized?

There are five bits of eggshell in the back of the food box. Anna was stolen from her family on Sunday, so today must be Friday, *erev Shabbat*. Her mother and sister will be roasting fish with vegetables for the evening meal. It is Anna's job to prepare the *caponata* of eggplant, peppers, and olives, and the *torta salata* of spinach and almonds, but today Allegrezza will have to do it, or Savta Rachele.

She knows that this afternoon she will endure yet another cleric, another sermon sure to persuade her, delivered by an even more esteemed excellency. And at night, when the oil in the lamp burns out, she will drown in darkness. While her family sleeps, safely locked behind ghetto walls, she will be awoken again and again by robed strangers, men who threaten her, tease her, who find new, ever crueler ways to entrap her. No shred of moonlight dares to enter through the barred window. Not even the occasional flare of a passing torch finds its way into this dark place.

When she is blinded by the night, her fears attack her like a pack of wolves, growling, baring their teeth, eyes glowing in the dark, and she cannot run fast enough to escape them. Jaws snap all around her, hungry for her soul. She tries to reason with herself, to tell herself that she is clever enough, strong enough to resist the wolves for seven more days.

A Jew who comes within forty rods of this convent will be given three lashes and fined one hundred *scudi*. It is even forbidden for a Jew to look up at the windows from a distance. She cannot hope that her parents will visit her here, nor can she write or receive a message, but she does not doubt that her family is fighting for her. Tatà, Dod Angelo, and the other memunim must have written to Vicegerent de' Rossi. They must have appealed to the Tribunal of the Inquisition. Tatà is a member of the ruling Congregation of Sixty. He has Catholic friends—the clients whose palaces he furnishes, the *ragioniere* who comes to the shop to help with the books, the *notaio* whose seal is on every family document, every betrothal contract, every will and testament. These Catholic men came with their families to Tranquillo's wedding. They visit the temple on holidays to listen to the music, defying their pope. Her father will have asked them to help her.

Cicero wrote, *"Dum spiro, spero."* While I breathe, I hope. At night, when terror stalks her, in the morning, when despair awakens her, she reminds herself that she is being foolish. In seven more days, she will be at home in the safety of the ghetto. She will make herself a new gown for her sister's wedding. She already has a length of striped Turkish silk for the skirt and a roll of Venetian lace to edge the sleeves.

The del Monte women have been embroidering Allegrezza's *dònara* for months, sitting on chairs outside the door to the shop when the sun shines, at the kitchen table when it rains. They are embellishing tablecloths, pillowcases and nightdresses. With the smallest of stitches, Savta Rachele embroidered the Castelnuovo family crest on the sheet that would cover them on their wedding night, and when she told Allegrezza that she must welcome her husband into her body, they all laughed, pointing at Allegrezza, who was bent over, hiding her face in her hands. Anna thinks of these things, and for a few minutes, the tightness in her throat relaxes, then the fear that she may never see her home again creeps back into her head, and the hungry wolves growl and bare their teeth.

This afternoon, Allegrezza will complain that she

must do Anna's chores as well as her own. She will set the sabbath table with a clean white cloth, polish the candlesticks and the cutlery, and wrap the braided bread in an embroidered napkin. Mammà will put a tight lid on the *chaminìmmi* of meatballs, rice, and lentils, then she will bury it in the ashes to keep it warm for the sabbath when it is forbidden to cook or even to make a fire. As the sun sets, the smell of spices will fill the kitchen, and the trumpeter will walk through the streets playing the call to sabbath.

Anna remembers the sound of his trumpet so well she can summon it now in the silence of this cell. She tells herself she is a little wren, flying over the ghetto, following the trumpeter as he winds his way through the shadowy streets, looking down on the merchants as they close their shops, on Jacob the Jeweler as he carefully rolls his precious wares into their black velvet cases. She flies to the Scòla dei Siciliani and watches the *gabbai* fill the silver lamps with oil. From the rafters, she watches Tatà and Tranquillo sway in prayer, facing the Ark of the Torah. And after the final "*amein*," she watches the congregation crowd together, shaking hands, smiling, *buon shabbat, buon shabbat.* Good sabbath. She flies above Tatà and Tranquillo as they walk home, talking and laughing, perches on a windowsill to watch Mammà say the blessing as she lights the candles. After Tatà blesses the wine, she hears Savta Rachele tell Allegrezza to serve the caponata.

Alone in her cell, Anna pulls her shawl over her head and pretends to light candles, waves her palms over the flames three times and covers her eyes, whispering, *Baruch atoi Adonai, Eloheinu melech ha'olam asher kidishanu bimitz v'tav v'zivanu l'hadlich, ner shel Shabbat.* Blessed art Thou, oh Lord our God, King of the Universe, who has sanctified us and commanded us to light the sabbath candles.

The button-seller carefully rolls up the scrap of cloth where her wares were displayed and places it in her sack. She scours the cobblestones to be sure not a single button, not a single bit of lace has been lost. She can hear the sabbath trumpeter in the distance, announcing that the sun is setting and that all work must cease. It has been a good day. Jews never touch money on the sabbath, so they do all their shopping on Friday before the first star appears in the sky. Tonight, she will have a bit of chicken from the *Gemiluth Chasadim,* turnips and greens and bread. She stands up and brushes the dust and dirt from the back of her skirt. She must hurry before the shops close. She has enough coins to buy candles, and even a few more to buy wine.

DUSK. THE hour when Jews prepare their minds for the sabbath. The demon priest knows this and has chosen this moment to torment Anna while she is weak with longing for home. When he arrived, there was still light at the window, and now the candle in his lantern is burning low. The demon must think that if he talks long enough, he will talk her into surrender. But she will not be a trapped animal, forced to listen to his endless preaching. His words bounce off the walls of the cell. They fall onto the floor. They cannot touch her because she has flown away. She is with her family at the sabbath table,

Mammà, Tatà, Allegrezza, Savta Rachele, Tranquillo, and Ester. It has become dark in the room, but they have been talking and laughing too much to notice until Mammà gets up to light the lamps. Savta Rachele leans over her enormous bosom and says, "This demon priest reminds me of an old story." When Savta starts telling a story everyone stops talking to listen. "A famous preacher came to speak at the kal. He talked and talked, and he was sure that he'd had a great success with the people. The next day, he discovered that the head rabbi had been there to hear him. So, the preacher went to the rabbi and asked what he thought of the sermon.

"The rabbi said, 'After I heard you speak, I couldn't sleep all night!'

"'You were so moved?'

"'No,' the rabbi replied, 'but when I sleep during the day, I can never sleep at night.'"

B'adonai! Anna thinks she must have gone mad. She is laughing aloud. The demon has a little bucket full of water, which he claims is holy, and he is sprinkling it on the floor, on the food box, the chair, the bed. It is the funniest thing she has ever seen. She cannot stop laughing at him.

He whirls about, splashing her face. The water burns her cheeks, blisters her skin. She is caught in the midst of a blaze, but still, she cannot stop laughing.

HE IS gone. She has laughed him away, and she is still laughing, laughing as though her heart has broken. If she does not stop laughing at once, her laughter will turn to tears, and she will cry forever. She wipes her eyes with the palms of her hands and falls back on the bed, rocking from side to side, laughing.

The door moans on its hinges, warning her. Three priests parade into the barren cell, forming a dark-robed wall before her, and her laughter vanishes. She cowers on the narrow bed, her elbows on her knees, her hands on her head. The priests stare at her, eyes full of pity. The one who talks swings his lantern across her eyes, blinding her with the light. He says that he is called the Parish Priest, but they are all alike to her, and she is too sick to listen to their threats and lies. *Baruch atoi adonai.* She begs her God to remove these priests. "If You will not grant me peace, oh Lord, grant me silence."

One after another, the goim lecture her, hour after hour, all afternoon, all evening, and now it is the middle of the night. If she could bear to touch this Parish Priest's vile flesh, she would strangle him. "Stop! Stop! Stop!" she screams. "*Basta!* Enough! I will never believe in anything but the religion of my parents."

Perhaps her God has heard her. Perhaps her screaming has scared the priests away. The door sighs as it closes behind them.

She stares into the darkness. Her body trembles under the great weight of grief. Terror steals her breath. She needs her mother, her father, her brother, her sister, Savta Rachele. She has never been away from them before. She has never been alone. She listens for their voices. Mammà's voice, even her angry voice, would be a comfort now. She prays for an instant of Mammà's scolding, a split second of Savta Rachele's roiling laughter. She listens and listens, and finally, she hears her father's voice, low and calm. "Good night, my Channà, good night fijama." Her eyes close. Her breath slows.

~

WHAT IS it? What is it now? Again, the door cries out as it opens, again they have come to berate her. How can she put up her hair when the pin falls from her shaking fingers? What has become of her shawl? Her hands rush to her mouth. *Keep my soul, for I am godly. O Thou my God, save Thy servant who trusts in Thee.*

Satan himself is staring at her.

His savage eyes rip her apart. A fiend has been sent from the Catholic hell to punish the impudent Jewess who laughed at one priest and screamed at another. If this is in fact, a man, it is the ugliest man who has ever lived. Hairy warts, motley purple and black, sprout from odd corners of his face, the middle of his forehead, the tip of his malformed nose, the corner of a misshapen eye. His teeth are too big for his mouth, his pulpous lips unable to contain them.

Anna wraps herself in the blanket, her back to the wall, her eyes closed, her hand in the pocket of her skirt, her fingers stroking the silk bag that contains Savta Rachele's amulet.

The fiend spits as it spews words. "Perhaps you believe that your *duricia*, your stupid Jewish obstinance will force us to send you home. But you are mistaken. Get that out of your head. You will remain in our hands until you become like us and believe in the one true god as we do. You think you will escape us with your silence, but you will not. You will end your days in this convent, without hope of ever seeing your mother or your father or any of your family again."

Do not listen, Channà. Do not listen. He is lying, trying to frighten you into submission, but you are not an ignorant girl from the Strada della Fiumara who would trade her soul for a new dress. You are a del Monte. Your mother is a Zevi. You will leave this place. You will.

He has bent his monstrous head over her and is screaming into her ear, as if he could blast all thoughts from her mind.

"Say something! I swear to you that I will call on the Sacred College of Cardinals. I will call on the holy pontiff himself. You will not win this struggle. Perhaps you are counting the days until you are released because you think you have been denounced, but you have not been. No! You have been offered. Do you know what that is, stubborn Jewess? Your soul has been offered to the Church, and we mean to collect it. You will stay here for a quarantine of forty days, and if that is not enough, you will stay here for another forty days and another and another, until all your days are gone, and you are buried where none of your Jewish family can find your grave.

"With this holy water, I convert you by force!" He throws his head back, grinning, his terrible eyes wide in triumph. The water pounds Anna's head, pours over her forehead into her eyes. She bats her hands around her face.

His words are daggers in her chest, her stomach. The pain is terrible. It cannot be. It cannot be. Perhaps he is stronger than she is, but she can scream louder.

"Neither my face nor my body will ever accept a drop

of this water. I am Jewish! Your water means no more than if a dog peed on me!"

He says nothing, nothing! He takes a cord from the bag he wears tied around his waist, the sort of cord they use to hang a man by the arms in the Campo de' Fiori.

"This is the crown," he says, and he begins to circle her forehead with the cord. "This is the chain that has attached your heart to our faith, and this water, which I pour over you, has the power to quench the infernal fire that is prepared for you and for all Jews. Nothing will cool the flames of hell but to accept this holy water with love.

"This is the crown.... This is the water.... This is the crown.... This is the water...." He says it over and over again, an incantation. He can repeat it forever, drown her in his cursed water, and still, she will be a Jew.

He is kneeling now; his voice is softer. "I will pray for you, so that your mind will be raised from the dark clouds and your intellect from the dusky shadows of your beliefs."

She wonders that this hideous man thinks it is possible that he has converted her, that she will forsake her family, her religion, because he pours water over her and circles her head with rope. He is like the crazy beggar who waits at the Gate of Severus, repeating the *Schemà* over and over again, night and day. And she knows that she could never believe in the benevolence of a faith that resorts to such cruel means of persuasion.

SHE HAS slid off the bed onto the floor. Her mouth is dry. Her lips stick to her teeth. Panic rises from the pit of her stomach and burns her throat. She is trapped in an endless black tunnel. Forty days and then another forty days. She has been offered, like a biblical goat to be sacrificed on an altar, the *sa'ir la-'Aza'zel*, the goat burdened with the sins of all Jews.

Oh Lord, redeem me from the oppression of man, and I shall observe They commandments. Please, dear God, have pity. If thou seeth me, prevent me from succumbing to weakness.

She was a good Jewish daughter at home with her family, her future laid out before her like a tapestry pattern drawn in ink, waiting to be woven, the colors already chosen. It has been written in the Book of Life that she will be married, that she will have children, that she will cook and sew, care for her family, dress nicely to go to the kal, pray and gossip with her friends. The threads of the tapestry will weave in and out, the holidays come and go, year after year. Savta Rachele will die and be buried. Then Tatà, Mammà. They will bury her brother, her sister. They will bury her, and her funeral procession will be dark and silent. Her children, her grandchildren, their grandchildren will live as Jews have always lived. How is it possible that she is imprisoned in this Catholic convent, without hope of escape? This should not be happening. This is wrong!

On the night she was taken from her home, the Bargello Squazzo pointed his pistol at Allegrezza as they stood behind the kitchen table. "Which one is Anna del Monte?" Anna pried her mother's hands from her waist and stepped forward.

"I am Channà del Monte," she said, insisting on her Hebrew name. "I will come with you, but first I would like to change my dress."

Her father took her hand, "Channà," he said, "listen to me...." The Bargello Squazzo swirled around and thrust his pistol into Tatà's chest. Every morning and every evening in this cell, Anna thanks the God of Abraham that her father was not killed.

A Jew can be denounced for saying anything that might be construed as an interest in Catholicism. Someone claims to have overheard something. He goes to the Inquisition and swears before a notary that this person or that one wishes to convert. The Jew is carried off to this place, or to the place where they keep the men, and detained for twelve days. They say it is to determine whether the desire to convert is genuine. Now Anna knows that is not true, and she understands why so few Jews ever return to the ghetto.

To be offered is another thing. To be offered is to be imprisoned in this place for a quarantine, forty days of indoctrination. A man who converts to Catholicism is expected to offer as a gift to the Church his wife, his children, his grandchildren, any person over whom he has some claim of authority.

The ghetto writhes with stories. The convert Samuele de Nepi offered his pregnant wife, and although she managed to withstand forty days of this torture without succumbing, she was kept here until her child was born, so that they could take it from her, sprinkle it with water and proclaim it Catholic. She had no choice but to convert or lose her baby forever.

When Davide Sermoneta converted, he offered the four-year-old daughter of his dead brother. The little girl was dragged away from her howling mother and baptized. Nearly every family in the ghetto has a story. If a Jewish child is five minutes late coming home, his mother dies a thousand deaths imagining that he has been kidnapped by the pope's sbirri.

Anna never thought this could happen to her. Not to a del Monte, a Zevi. She was obedient and calm when they came to take her away, assuming she would be permitted to put on a clean dress, gather a few things, and walk with dignity from the only home she had ever known. But sbirri are the coarsest of men. Any woman, Jewish, Muslim, or Catholic, will cross the street to avoid passing close to them. Two men, who ought not dare even speak to an unmarried woman, grabbed her by the arms. And she knew what it is to be a prisoner.

She could hear the crowd outside before she got through the door. Tranquillo and Ester were in the street, barred from entering their building. They called her name over and over. *Channà! Channà!* She tried to twist her head to look at them, but the sbirri began to run, their hands gripping her upper arms so tightly she was sure they would break. Her feet, clothed only in house slippers, dragged over the cobblestones. Her captors rushed her through the Gate of Severus into the Piazza Giudea and threw her into a waiting carriage, which took off at once while a crowd of Jews ran behind it, shouting insults and throwing loose cobblestones, trash, anything they could find. The two sbirri sat on either side of her, grasping and pinching, so that she was forced to curl her body into a ball to avoid them.

Why is she here? Who has done this? Who has betrayed her? Who? She sorts through the faces of every person she has ever known, turning them over one by one, like Savta Rachele's Tarot cards. Who has been recently converted? Who has a claim over her? Who? What aunt or uncle, what cousin, however distant, could have offered her?

She shuffles the cards, reshuffles. There are seventy-eight cards in the deck, twenty-two cards in the Major Arcana, twenty-two letters in the Hebrew alphabet, twenty-two paths connecting the Sefirot. If she turns over twenty-two cards, the last card will reveal who has betrayed her. First, the top card. The Star of David, an unblinking eye in its center. She turns the cards over in her mind as she remembers them. The queen of swords, her head above the clouds, her weapon raised. The queen glances at Anna, seeing the invisible, then floats off into the night. The knight of pentacles arrives on horseback bringing sorrow. The page of cups, the ace of wands. Earth, air, fire, water, the sun, the moon. The moon! Darkness into light. The moon and the howling wolf.

The fishmongers at the market outside the Pescaria Gate hate Jews. They listen to their conversations hoping to hear something they can report to the Inquisition. If one of them overheard something Anna said without thinking, he might have denounced her. But she was not denounced, she was offered. To be offered to the Church, to become an unwilling gift requires more than an overheard conversation. The giver must have some authority over the person. Who? Who had the power to offer her?

Cards fly through the air, shuffled by the wind, tossed about, blurred. Faces leer at her. Hands reach for her. Colors and shapes swirl in the dark. The twentieth card. The magician stands beside his table. The twenty-first card, the king of wands sits on his desert throne, a lizard at his feet. The king is *chaya*, life. Again and again, Savta Rachele has told Anna that she is incorrigible, that she is headstrong. And always, she tells her that these attributes will save her. One more card, the twenty-second card. Anna's mind searches for this final card but they are all a jumble, spinning, falling. And *badanai!* The card of Satan who perverts what is good, Satan the opposer. Satan on his throne, clawed feet, dark wings. Horns sprout from his head in place of a crown. She has seen the man who wears this face on the streets of the ghetto, talking with Tatà. She has seen him in her family's shop. Satan wears the face of that imbecile Sabato Coen who lives with his mother and sister in the filth of the Strada della Fiumara at the edge of the Tiber. Only the charity of the *Gemulit Chasadim* saves them from starvation. Sabato Coen is a *scìneco* who cannot even read his prayer book. Suppose he came to see her father, hoping for a dowry that would lift his family from misery. Tatà would never have allowed him to marry her.

Suppose this Coen converted. He has nothing to barter but his soul and the Church will pay a hundred scudi for it. If Coen has been baptized, he will be expected to offer other Jewish souls to the Church. Why has he chosen her? Who would believe that illiterate scum has authority over her, a del Monte? He will have told any lie in order to offer her.

She is to be locked in this nightmare for forty days and forty more. A quarantine. Moses spent forty days in heaven when he received the Torah. The Great Flood lasted forty days. The Jews wandered in the wilderness for forty years. The ritual *mikveh* bath must be filled with forty measures of water. At forty days from conception, a baby is well-formed in its mother's womb. A Jew must reach the age of forty to properly understand the Torah.

How many Jewish women have come through the doors of this place never to be heard of again? Is she really so much stronger? Who is she to withstand endless sermons, reassurances, promises, threats? She is so weary. Her mind is no longer well.

There are a thousand stories of Jews who have been taken from the ghetto and brought to this place. She saw it happen with her own eyes on the evening of *Tisha b'Av*, the anniversary of the destruction of Jerusalem, when all mourning rites are observed. The five kals of the Cinque Scòla were emptying out after services. The *Scòla Catalana*, the *Scòla Castigliana*, the *Scòla del Tempio*, the *Scòla Nova*—and the *Scòla Siciliani* where the del Monte family has attended services for generations. The men were milling about, joking and gossiping, while the women started for home so that they could put the meal on the table.

They had just crossed the piazza when they saw four sbirri coming through the Gate of Severus, pistols drawn. Too fascinated, too horrified to move, they huddled together. The memunim rushed over, but no one has ever succeeded in stopping an abduction once it has begun. The sbirri pounded on the ancient wooden door of the fourth house on the Strada della Rua. When there was no immediate reply, they easily broke the door down.

A moment later, one of them came out with Devora Panzieri slung over his shoulder like a bag of rags. She was kicking and striking his back with her fists, still wearing the blue silk gown she saves for holidays, her blond hair undone, hiding her face. Devora, Anna's friend, who not ten minutes before had been whispering and giggling in the women's gallery. Good, beautiful Devora was no more to these men than a common whore they could grab and touch as they liked, a piece of merchandise, a thing.

They carried her through the ghetto gates and threw her into a waiting carriage, while her mother ran after them, tripping on her skirts, screaming that they were taking the wrong girl. Anna watched the carriage race away, never imagining that this would one day happen to her. She thought she was too innocent, her family too well-respected.

The next morning, neighbors called to one another from the windows. Rumors rumbled through the ghetto. Tranquillo came into the kitchen to tell his family what he'd heard at the scòla. Mammà wiped her hands on her apron. Allegrezza put down her knife. Savta Rachele hurried in from next door, insisting that Tranquillo had to wait until she had settled herself.

"This is what I know," he said finally, stealing a piece of the carrot Allegrezza had been chopping. "That Devora Panzieri and Matteo Rosato are in love is generally acknowledged by everyone in the ghetto with the possible exception of Devora's parents. That Matteo wants to marry her goes without saying, but he has not yet summoned the courage to speak to her father. After all, what can he give her? He has little money, no room of his own where he could bring a bride.

"Devora is a nice girl who would never dare to leave her house unescorted or be seen talking with a man, but she and Matteo wrote love notes. Each night while the family was asleep, she listened for him to whistle softly under her window, then she lowered her note in a basket on a rope. He took it, placed his own note in the basket, and she raised it.

"A perfect system, until Devora's mother realized what was happening. She took the basket away and only brought it out in the mornings so that she could lower it to buy vegetables from the street sellers without having to come down the stairs. I have this from her brother, Giacomo, so you can believe it. That night, when Devora heard Matteo's whistle, having no basket to lower, she threw her love note out the window, a very foolish thing to do. At night, the ghetto is darker than Lot's cave. No torchbearers patrol the streets, and no Jew can afford to leave a lamp burning. Matteo searched and searched for the note, but it was hopeless. He told himself he had only imagined that he saw a white scrap flying out the window and went home."

Tranquillo surveyed his little audience. "So. You understand what happened? Allegrezza, you look like you are about to faint. Sit down.

"Early the next morning, one of Cardinal Ruffo's lackeys came to the ghetto looking for trouble, and he found Devora's note on the ground. He read it, then hid himself where he could watch until she appeared at the window. When he saw her, he was so amazed at her beauty, he fell in love with her. *Beh*, she's a good-looking girl. Not that my sisters are any less beautiful, but you know, Devora has such huge, bright eyes.

"The lackey took Devora's note to Cardinal Ruffo, pretending that the letter had been written not to Matteo, but to him. Listen well, dear sisters. That will teach you to address a letter to '*amore mio*' without mentioning a name. The lackey told the cardinal that Devora wanted to become Catholic so that she could marry him, but her parents prevented it. Had she not written that she dreamed only of the day when her father would allow her to become his wife? The cardinal was delighted at the chance to acquire another Jewish soul, especially the soul of a healthy young woman who would be sure to breed lots of Catholic children. So, he sent the sbirri to take her by force. This part I heard from Dod Angelo who has already gone with the memunim to the Office of the Inquisition."

For weeks afterwards, the memunim petitioned the vicegerent. Their Christian lawyer petitioned the Tribunal of the Inquisition, but because Cardinal Ruffo had ordered her abduction himself, he refused to hear them.

Months passed. Devora's sister, Malzadò, became so ill she never left her bed. Matteo Rosato wandered the alleys of the ghetto tearing at his clothes like a madman. One day, they heard that after many weeks in the Catacumeni, Devora had surrendered to the eager hands of the Catholic Church. It was rumored that Cardinal Ruffo acted as godfather at her baptism, and that he found a Catholic husband for her, a man who worked for the post. Malzadò died soon afterwards. No Jew ever saw Devora again.

∾

ANNA IS on the stone floor, shivering in the dark. her hips, her legs, her knees, her elbows ache. If this desolate place is to be her prison for forty days and forty more, she must learn to live here. If this straw pallet is to be her bed, she must learn to sleep on it. If this cell is to be her only home, she had better find the courage to undress for the night, to bare her collarbone and undo her hair. When they come, she will wrap herself in the blanket. She will sit with closed eyes, and it will be as though she had died. They will scream at her, pour water on her, but she will not hear them, and she will not answer them.

In the name of Adonai, the God of Israel, may the angel Michael be at my right, the angel Gabriel at my left, in front of me the angel Uriel, behind me the angel Raphael and above my head, the Sh'khinah, the Divine Presence.

T HE PRIORESS is flitting about like a delighted hostess, ordering the nuns to place a chair here or there. Six men in white cassocks with rosary beads looped around their waists have crowded into the cell, and creeping in behind them, a woman. Anna's hand flies to her mouth and she bites down on her fist. The woman looks cleaner than Anna has ever seen her, in a new gown of rose-colored linen with lace at the edges of the neckline and sleeves, her hair curled in ringlets and neatly pinned to the top of her head. The sister of Sabato Coen, the dirty, ignorant liar who, Anna now has no doubt, condemned her to this place. Sabato Coen— may his name and memory be erased from the Book of Life—has offered them both to the Catholic Church.

It is Saturday morning, the day of the sabbath, when Anna should be seated in the gallery of the Scòla Siciliano, dressed beautifully to honor the Holy One, blessed be His name. Instead, she is in this airless cell with Perla Coen—she would not even bother to spit on her—and six circumcised friars with Jewish faces. Why do they always come in groups? Are the others here to learn from the one who speaks, or to spy on him?

Anna watches their mouths, which are always more interesting than their dull eyes. She watches their lips, their teeth, their tongues, their sneers, their surprised smiles, the tightness that betrays their frustration or their smugness. Their eyes are dark, empty. So, she watches their mouths.

The one who speaks has been honored with a seat on a hard wooden chair. Perla Coen sits behind him beside the prioress, while five others stand in a tight crowd surrounding Anna, suffocating her. The one who speaks calls her his sister. His lips are the color of eggplant. His voice drips with honey. He wants to know if she believes in the God of Abraham. Does she believe in the God of our Fathers? Does she believe in the Almighty?

Of course, she believes in God. He knows she does. But he cannot compel her to say the word. He cannot trick her into saying "yes."

He raises his voice. "Why do you refuse to answer me? I have not asked anything that might endanger you. I only wish to know if you believe in the God of Isaac and Jacob and in all the prophets, because we also believe in these things."

His mouth repeats a lie that he has been told, a lie he tells himself day after day. He has been taught the lie that Catholicism is an improved version of Judaism with the added benefit of a messiah, and he has been told that it is his job to teach this lie to her.

"Do you not believe, my sister, that we adore the same god your rabbis have instructed you to worship?"

She thinks they must pay this Jewish priest for each soul he steals. Perhaps they move him up the priestly ladder with each life he ruins.

"You think we pray to certain idols and images, but to us, these are not idols. They are symbols of the saints to whom we pray for the salvation of our souls. You Jews refuse to accept the true god, the true messiah, because you will not recognize that he is the true redeemer. And so, you first brutally martyred him and then put him to death on the cross, and yet it is to him that I pray, that he may enlighten you and give you the grace to recognize him and believe in him."

He calls his own people "you Jews." Does he think that because they have said a few Latin words and sprinkled water on his head, he is no longer Jewish? Does he believe that they have severed the roots of his soul, planted five thousand years ago?

He says, "All the chatter of your rabbis, who endlessly expound on your Torah, only obscures the light of the true faith. But they will understand when they have been condemned to the inferno for their refusal to believe, and so will you if you fail to hear my prayers today. You Jews dare to say that we worship a god different from yours, but that is a falsehood."

Does this young convert expect her to believe that he knows better than all the rabbis who have pondered the infinite for century upon century?

"Your rabbis falsify passages of scripture and interpret them as they wish against the commandments of God.

May God forgive me if I want to burn first the Talmudists and then all their books and false writings, which are the cause of the scourging of your Jewish souls."

So, he wants to burn the Talmud, the book of instruction, the collected commentaries of the wisest rabbis. But the Inquisition confiscated and burned every copy of the Talmud long before she was born. Again, last year the sbirri came into the ghetto, searching house by house for forbidden Hebrew books. The memunim tried to reason with them, but the only concession they were granted was that a rabbi was permitted to accompany the invaders in order to translate the Hebrew titles, which none of them were able to decipher. When they came to the del Monte house, they found volumes of Aristotle, Cicero, Ovid, and Horace. They found a copy of the Midrash and the Jewish prayer book, the Siddur, in a silver box embossed with the family seal.

This circumcised priest has nothing to fear from the Talmud. It has ceased to exist in Rome. The only remaining copies are in the library of the Vatican.

Does he think the Church accepts him as a good Catholic? Does he think they trust him? Does he wonder why he is here in this place, berating Jews who need to be shown the light, instead of celebrating mass in one of the great basilicas?

He is threatening her now. She knows this practice. It begins with a sweet voice then escalates to a harsh one. He says, "You will accept the light of the Son of God, or you will send your soul to perdition, like the souls of all the other Jews who make excuses before God on the Day of Judgement. Think on this well. And we will leave you in peace."

But there is no peace. Locked in this cell, she struggles with despair. *Adh-'ânâh Adonai, How long, oh Lord, how long? How long will Thou hide Thy face from me? How long will my enemy be exalted over me?*

S UNDAY IS a busy day in the ghetto. While the rest of Rome is closed for the Catholic sabbath, the Strada della Rua is crowded with gentiles who come to browse, to stroll, to eat Jewish pastries and drink kosher wine. Soon the del Monte antique shop will open, but at dawn, Belfiore and Benedetto are still lying on their thick woolen mattress. The carved mahogany bed has been in the del Monte family for more generations than anyone knows, a relic of a time when they were among the wealthiest families in Rome. The four bedposts are each topped with finials in the shape of pomegranates, the headboard engraved with the del Monte family crest.

Belfiore is watching her husband, wondering if he has slept at all. He is on his back, staring up at the red brocade canopy. "Baruch," she says softly. She calls him by his Hebrew name, Baruch, Benedetto, blessed one. "Our Channà will come back to us. We must have faith."

He turns his eyes towards her. "I woke you, Dodi." He calls her "Dodi," the Hebrew word for "beloved."

"No, no," she says. "A mother does not sleep when her right arm has been torn from her body, her heart ripped from her breast."

"You think I have not done enough, Dodi. I see the way you look at me. You think I am a weak husband, a useless father. What is a man who cannot protect his own daughter, who does nothing while the sbirri put their filthy hands on her and drag her away?"

"*Aùh*! Baruch. What does it matter if I think you are as strong as Goliath? Tell me, are you the pope who made these laws? Are you the cardinal who heads the Inquisition, the judge who presides over the Tribunal? Are you Vicegerent de' Rossi who makes every decision without first consulting his conscience? My Baruch, you are a good and honest Jew, and to be a good and honest Jew in this world is to be at a terrible disadvantage. This is the price we pay for refusing to believe what we know cannot possibly be true. Our Channà is smart, educated, stubborn. Stop crying for her and start crying for the poor frustrated priests who try to steal her soul. Now I am going to wash and dress." She buries her nose against his neck.

"You are wrong, Dodi. To be a good and honest Jew is not to be powerless."

She has no reply. She has been married long enough to know when to speak and when to be silent. For twenty-seven years, his face has been the first thing she has seen every morning, and the last thing she has seen every evening. Her life is grafted onto his. She grows and blooms and wilts with him.

In the next room, she bathes her hands and face and whispers the morning prayers before dressing. Then she lights the *folcarola* and fills the kettle with water from the jug, lowers herself onto a bench and tucks the corners of her shawl into her bodice.

Her daughter Channà is eighteen years old. Eighteen and locked away in that place. When she, herself, was eighteen, her mother gave her a green velvet cloak trimmed with satin ribbons and asked her what she would think of marrying Baruch del Monte. "He is a nice-looking boy, educated. The family has a good business. His father said something to your father."

It was her duty to at least consider him. She had seen him all her life, watched him in the streets with the other boys going back and forth on the Strada della Rua. Now he was twenty-four years old and ready to marry. Belfiore's father invited him to their rooms. She looked him over carefully. He was not too tall, not too short, clear complexion, green eyes, dark beard, strong brow. She imagined his cheek touching hers, his lips, his hands stroking her body. They sat and talked while her mother kept busy with her sewing, pretending not to eavesdrop. He seemed gentle and kind, intelligent. He had read a great many books. He said he was glad that she loved to read. He said that he wanted a wife who could do more than bake a sponge cake.

So, she consented to the marriage. The fathers negotiated. There were many clauses in the betrothal contract but no discord between the two families. The del Monte and the Zevi were both prosperous by ghetto standards. Both families allowed their daughters some education.

Both families had been congregants at the Scòla Siciliana for more than three hundred years.

The groom's father agreed to pay a sum equal to one-third of the dowry her father offered, and the four parents signed the contract before a Christian notary so that no questions could be asked by anyone. Then Belfiore's father took her hand and placed it on Benedetto's to accept the ring. She looked at her fiancé's tear-filled eyes, his unquestioning smile, and she was happy.

When the moon waned, the great Rabbi Corcos himself read the vows under the wedding canopy while seven torchbearers walked around the couple seven times. Baruch drank from a cup of wine, passed it to his bride, and what was left in the cup, he poured onto the floor. Then he threw the empty cup into the air, and as it crashed, breaking into a hundred pieces, the guests shouted, "Mazel tov!"

After the roast capon, the cured meats and the cake, men danced with women, women danced with women, men danced with men. Everyone danced with the children. The *signore del gioco* led them all in riddles. The *confraternità Gemilut Chassadim* presented a play depicting the couple's happy future. Belfiore was carried aloft by the crowd, laughing, a little tipsy, thrilled to be the center of so much attention, but deep in her belly she was afraid. Her old life was over, her new life, a mystery.

Baruch del Monte was almost a stranger when he climbed into bed beside her that night, but he did his duty gently, and she did hers. They lived with his parents, 'sandro and Rachele, discretely circling each other, sharing the occasional smile, the furtive glance. When they were alone, his hands reached for her. He liked to stroke her head, to caress her cheek. She liked to rub her nose in the place where his neck met his shoulder. She admired his cleverness, his humor, his hard work, his consummate knowledge of the Torah. And that was enough. She thought this must be the love between a man and a wife, and every day she thanked the God of Abraham that Benedetto del Monte had chosen to marry her. He was the warm cloak that enfolded her life. His was the strong hand that led her up the mountain towards the sun. And the years passed.

The day his father died, he came into their room and closed the door. She looked at his crumpled body, and for the first time, she saw not a husband but a man. He was no longer her prophet, her Solomon, Moses, and Elijah. He was a boy trembling in grief. They had begotten three children, but she had never seen his body, nor he hers. At night, they undressed shyly, privately. Clothing separated them, even when they made love. But in his helpless sorrow, he was naked.

She stood there not moving, afraid that her comforting touch might embarrass him. The sight of his grief had tapped an enormous reservoir buried within her, and a torrent of love flowed toward him. He lifted his face. "Forgive me, Dodi," he said. "You should not see me like this." She squeezed his arm as she left the room. "Maybe a little glass of wine," she said.

Now the kettle rattles and boils. In the next room, Baruch snores. Belfiore hides her face and weeps, a dry, silent weeping she can instantly mask with a smile.

⌀

ONE KILOMETER and a world away, Anna del Monte is praying. The nun's shift she has been given to sleep in falls to her ankles and covers her arms. Her feet are bare on the cold floor, and her hands, accustomed to holding a prayer book, lay empty on her breast. She slept only a short, exhausted slumber before she awoke in the dark. Forty days and forty more of ostentatiously dressed clerics tormenting her with grotesque versions of Old Testament stories she has loved since childhood. Forty nights and forty more of shabby priests parading into this little cell, blinding her with their lanterns, terrifying her. Forty days and nights, trapped in this bare, dim room, with no view of the sky, the walls closing in on her.

But this morning when the dawn broke, she'd had enough of despair and weeping. And what use is there in tears? So, she began to pray, first sitting on the narrow straw bed, now pacing the cell, marking the limits of her confinement.

Hat·teh·ha·shem a·ze·ne·cha a·ne·ni. In thee Oh Lord, I found shelter and was not ashamed. Bow down Thy ear to me. Deliver me speedily. Be my strong rock, my fortress, my defense. Have mercy upon me, for I am in trouble. My eye wastes away with grief, yea, my soul and my body. Save me from these lions who do not eat my flesh but try to devour my soul.

Her face, pretty enough at rest, has become refulgent, animated by the Hebrew words she whispers on a thread of breath, brow knitted in concentration, green eyes raised as though searching for hope in the penumbra. As the gray dawn lifts the blackness of the cell, she rises from the depths of misery, floating on the sound of singing. *Paige lingua gloriosi. Carpers mysterium Sanguinisque pretiosi.* The nuns sing in Latin, the language of Ovid and Cicero, Horace and Virgil. How strange, these goim with their prayers of dead bodies and blood!

～

THE CURATE Cachèmme has honored her with another visit. Anna watches him grasp the arms of the upholstered chair as he settles his wide bottom on the cushion.

"Here I am, my daughter. I have come immediately from Saint Peter's Basilica. I awoke very early and spent two hours on my knees praying for your soul, and the good Lord has assured me that before the last bells have tolled on this day, you will see the light."

What a trial it must have been for this fat old man to spend so much time on his knees! She says, "I thank you, Monseigneur, but surely, your prayers are not enough to tear me away from my own religion. Such a miracle as that could never be the work of human hands. Your words are no more than all your idolatry, no more than your saints, which are painted by men from their own imaginings."

And she prepares herself for an enraged response to her insolent little speech.

But the curate speaks softly. "I do not come here in anger," he says.

She sees that in his eyes she is no more than a recalcitrant child in need of correcting, and she crosses her arms tightly across her chest, fighting an urge to slap him.

"Likewise, when we men of the cloth visit you to interrogate you or to preach to you, it is not simply to annoy you. If you have any doubts, tell me what they are so that I may explain everything to you. I am a theologian. I can dissolve any doubt whatever with my knowledge of the Sacred Scriptures. I want to win your heart using your own texts."

He leans back against the cushions of his chair, uncrosses and recrosses his thick ankles, then stares at her, waiting to lock her unwilling eyes with his before he continues. "I would like to show you clearly with the strength of the text of Jeremiah, which says: 'In Zion, God caused the solemn appointments and the sabbath to be forgotten.' So, you see that God no longer wished to make the sabbath on Saturday, but instead, wished that it be observed on Sunday."

Laughter bubbles in the back of her throat, but she keeps her face still and speaks to him as slowly and clearly as he has spoken to her. "I am sure that you are a theologian," she says, "but it is obvious to me that you lack the Divine Light, and having misunderstood the verse, you are hardly capable of explaining its allegorical meaning. If God did, indeed, say that he wished us to forget the feast days and the sabbath, he said so to *punish* us for the transgressions with which we have offended him since time immemorial. Because we failed to observe the sabbath and the sacred holidays, He wanted to punish us also on *those* days, withholding them from us. This is *precisely* what Jeremiah says."

For a moment, she is ashamed of her hubris. Her father would not like to hear his daughter speak so disrespectfully. The curate is a kind man, but she is a prisoner in this place. Why should she display the good manners of a guest?

The fat old man has some response. He is talking, but

she has stopped listening. She turns her head and counts the bricks on the wall opposite the cell window. How many big ones, how many dark ones, how many rows of bricks? Ancient bricks support new bricks, the present precariously balanced on so much history.

The curate raises his voice in an attempt to recapture her attention. "Since it has pleased God to deliver you into our hands in order to teach you the true faith, we have taken you from the filth of your ghetto and wish only to purify you with the baptismal waters."

He is saying that by abducting her from the sanctity of her family, they have rescued her from filth.

"Forgive me, Monseigneur, if I cannot agree with your suggestion. I was born a Jew and I will die a Jew, no matter what you say or how much water you sprinkle on me, because I know that a woman is a Jew by birth, and that a male makes a covenant with God through *brit mila*, circumcision. With His own voice, God commanded Abraham to make this covenant himself and with all his male offspring, so long as the earth exists. You will save yourself a great deal of trouble by returning me to the arms of my parents. Why should it matter to you whether my soul is damned or not?"

Again, she has been insolent, but what is this precious soul they are all so determined to save? Who owns it if not our Lord, blessed be His name? What is it that it can be converted, bartered, cleansed, saved? In the Torah, it is written that while there is life, the body and soul are one, and every living thing has a soul. What man has the right to meddle with the soul of another? And who is this curate to decide whether a soul is pure or not, saved or not? She knows that when she dies, her soul will return to God, and He will decide whether she has made good use of it while it was in her care.

HER HANDS are clasped behind her back but still they shake. She tenses every muscle in her body to hide her terror. Ten men have crowded into this cell—Curate Chiaccierone, the monstrous one they call the Parish Priest, another friar and six more, also priests—all of them reeking of death, leaving her without air to breathe.

The Parish Priest is making his usual incantations, sprinkling his water all over like a cat who sprays its stench everywhere. She no longer cares who wins or loses or what they think of her, but this priest has no right to drench her person without her permission.

She says, "Every ugly thing you do with your cursed water, with your sermons, is useless. The more you try to weaken me, the stronger I become, the more committed to my own faith. Your stupid water games do not impress me. These are the tricks of children. All I wish is to return to the arms of my honorable parents, and to live and die with them."

She clutches at her skirts as though to rip them apart. She screams, but the Parish Priest screams louder. Every nun, every neophyte, every imprisoned Jewess in the cloister must hear it.

The Parish Priest is hideous, his head thrown back, his eyes blazing, his mouth twisted. "Do not think you are going to return to your home! You may be here for forty days, or for twenty times forty days. I have been expressly ordered by the Sacred Congregation to teach you the doctrine and the other precepts of the Church in order to save your soul. Hear what I say! I have complete authority to do whatever I wish to bring about your conversion. And you speak of wanting to go home. You had better give up this foolish talk. Again, I repeat that you will never leave here, and I swear it."

Her knees have given way. She is crouching on the floor in the corner of the cell, one woman against Christ's army.

And now comes Perla Coen. That *desgrazzia, sciabbàdda*, that *porcheria* is making her way through the crowd of men who move aside for her like the parting of the Red Sea. She is all smiles and happiness, kneeling beside Anna who would rather endure the loathsome hands of ten uncircumcised men than this woman's perfidious fingers. Perla is stroking her head, whispering improper things about how glad she is in body and soul, and how sorry that she did not find this solution to her problems sooner. Anna is sure that this Perla is being fed as much as she likes every day, eating their *tarèffe*, their pig meat. Perla whispers that they have brought her here so that Anna can see how well she is, and then asks her why she does not do the same. She whispers, "If only you would listen to the Parish Priest and do as he says, even the goim would revere you and treat you as a lady. You would be courted by the princes and cavaliers of Rome instead of the scoundrels of the ghetto."

Anna tries to move away from this woman who restrains her with an arm around her shoulder. She says, "When you mention the scoundrels of the ghetto, you must include your own traitorous brother. Why should you care what becomes of me? They have already promised you a place in Paradise. If I convert, will they buy you a house and fill the cupboards with pretty things?"

Anna says these words to the stone floor. She cannot bring herself to look at this woman, but Perla still strokes her and whispers to her, until at last, having achieved nothing, she gets up and turns to leave, and they all follow behind her.

Alone in the cell, Anna counts eight bits of eggshell hidden in the food box. If there were a thousand bits, she would still be Channà del Monte, and she would still be a Jew.

I, the undersigned, having been shown the light of the Son of God, and having embraced the Catholic religion for the salvation of my soul, desiring that my betrothed wife, Anna del Monte, daughter of Benedetto del Monte and Belfiore Zevi, might also be enlightened, offer her to the Catholic Church.

In witness whereof, Rome this 19th day of April, 1749
In faith

(Sabato Coen)
Signed with a cross as the petitioner does not know how to write.

Sworn and witnessed before the notary of Cardinal Vicar Giovanni Antonio Guadagni and Vicegerent Ferdinando Maria de' Rossi

THE NUNS were awakened before the birds began to sing. In the dark, they performed the Angelus and Marian Consecration, the Office of Readings and Lauds. Then they hauled water, stoked the fires, cleaned their cells, and scrubbed every corner of the convent, whether it required cleaning or not. As the sky began to lighten, they removed their aprons and tidied themselves, fastened wimples and veils over tightly fitted caps to be properly dressed for the morning mass. Seated at long tables in the drafty refectory, they breakfasted on watery wine and hard bread, eating hungrily and silently while one of the sisters read aloud from the Gospels.

One hour after sunrise, a flock of novitiates in white habits files out into the street behind the black veil of Sister Innocènza. Most of them have required her counsel. Some of them have been heard weeping. They have been taught to sing in Latin, to memorize Latin prayers whose meaning they only dimly understand. They have been forbidden to speak the dialect of the ghetto they so recently left behind, and they have sworn to love the Savior. Each morning, Sister Innocènza reminds herself, and then the novitiates, to be grateful for their new lives. Their hands hidden in the wide sleeves of their habits, heads and voices low, they climb the Salita del Grillo from the Convento della Santissima Annunziata to the Casa dei Catacumeni, where they will begin the day's work.

ANNA HAS become too familiar with this cell, with these cracked and yellowing walls, the smell of musty straw, old wood and damp stone, the light that begs to enter through the barred window but is never granted permission. She is no longer horrified when she awakens here, wrenched from her comforting dreams.

Each morning, when the first light grazes her eyes, she lies still, gathering her strength. She thanks God for allowing her to live another day, no matter how terrible the next hours may be. She reminds herself to be grateful for these few moments of peace and silence and vows that though she may be imprisoned for forty, eighty, one-hundred-and-twenty days, or more, she will never resign herself to her fate.

The prioress has told her that the vicegerent has sent the best minds of the Church to change hers. She thinks this is just another lie, another attempt to flatter her into submission. As each of these great men fails to transform her into something she is not, another, even more erudite competitor appears, as though her soul were the prize in a tournament of words.

If she weakens, if she allows them to baptize her, she will lose everything she knows, everything she loves. A Jew who converts is watched, followed, never permitted to speak to another Jew, not even to a husband, a mother, a father, a child. She will be married off to a Catholic or forced to join an order like the young nuns in white robes who keep their eyes lowered each morning as they bring her a boiled egg and remove her chamber pot. The prioress says that she sends them to her cell for company, but they never speak.

This morning in her loneliness, when the nun in the black veil brings her a bit of bread and a pitcher of water, Anna asks if she knew her in the ghetto and waits, watches her nervously fingering the wooden rosary that hangs from her belt, swaying a little from side to side. She might have been surprised to be called out as a convert. Perhaps she hesitates because she is deciding if she dares to answer. Perhaps she has been forbidden to speak to a Jew.

"You are Anna del Monte." She says it in a voice so tremulous, Anna nearly reaches for her hand. "Everyone knew your family. Everyone in the ghetto. Here...."

Here they talk of her. Of course, they do. They flutter away from her cell when the bells chime, and whisper about her in the echoing corridors. They must have once been captives as she is, offered or denounced or in difficult circumstances. Something forced them to come here, to forsake the lives they were born to live.

Anna wants to ask this nun a thousand questions. Why is she here? Why is she a nun? Does she live in a cell like this one? Does she have paintings, carpets, a soft chair? Does she have books? Mammà often tells Anna that she is too forthright, that she asks too many questions, but she asks the nun one more. She tries to ask it sweetly.

"Why are you here in this *ingavuscìmme*? This prison? How did you come to leave your father and your mother?"

"The Lady Prioress is my mother."

"And your family?"

"My sisters in Christ are my family. I left that other life when I saw the light of the true religion, as I pray you will."

The nun studies Anna's face.

Anna thinks she may be hoping to trust her, so she motions to the bed, inviting her to sit beside her, but the nun does not notice or chooses to ignore her.

"I am Sister Innocènza." She is standing, looking down at Anna as though from a great height.

"But what was your name before?"

"Before don't matter. I've been reborn in the light of Jesus Christ, our Savior."

"Why are you a nun?

"I pray that someday you will understand why."

"Did no man ask to marry you?"

"I am the chosen bride of Jesus Christ."

Sister Innocènza holds up her hand, to show Anna the wedding band she wears. Anna thinks she must be talking with a madwoman, and that she must have asked too many questions, because the nun is moving towards the door.

The nun stops and turns, her black veil swishing behind her. "Three men asked for me."

Anna can believe that. This nun would not be a bad-looking girl if a few dark curls softened her face. The stiff white fabric of the wimple makes her complexion appear florid. Perhaps they allowed her to dress more attractively before she became a nun, prettied her up like that porcheria Perla Coen so she could find a real husband.

Sister Innocènza puts her hands inside the sleeves of her habit. "Rich patrons give us dowries. Men who marry converts don't have to pay certain taxes. The rector has letters from all sorts of men. He chooses one and the man comes to the convent.

"The prioress, or one of the older nuns, watches, and listens. The first one who came to look at me was old, a widower with two children. I could have had one like him in the ghetto, so I refused to marry him. You can do that. They don't force you. The next one was…"

"He was ugly?"

"He had a wart the size of a fist on the end of his nose."

Anna laughs and the nun laughs with her. For the first time since she was stolen from her home, she feels a little like herself. "And the third man?"

"He was not so bad, but he refused to marry me."

"How can you know that?"

"He never came back."

"So, you had no alternative but to become a nun?"

"When I became a nun, I saved my own soul and the souls of all my family. I was made to memorize the rites, the prayers. After two years, the cardinal vicar himself came to question me, and I took my vows in a ceremony with flowers and prayers and singing."

She seemed almost as delighted at the memory as a real wife remembering her wedding day. But Anna thinks she is not a real wife. She is a prisoner. "What did you promise when you took those vows? You agreed to lock yourself away forever."

"Did I? I took the vow of poverty. Poverty! Do you know what my life was in the ghetto? Have you seen how we live on the Strada della Fiumara? Every day when I climbed the stairs to our room, I tried not to step on a dead rat or a pile of *monghi*. The stairwell always stank. Every day I was hungry. If one of the confraternità come around with bread for us, we ate. In the convent, I have food every day. In the ghetto we lived in one room with one bed, my mother, my sister, and me. In the convent I have my own bed, clean clothes. I am warm, dry, fed."

Anna sees that this nun is an ignorant woman who speaks Italian badly. How she must struggle to avoid lapsing into the dialect of the ghetto! But she is so much more interesting than the endless parade of preachers who all say the same thing.

"I took the vow of chastity. What is chastity? My father pounded on my mother every Friday night when he come back from the kal. That will never happen to me. I doubt I will miss it.

"I took the vow of obedience. Does that word scare you? In the ghetto, I obeyed my father and when he died, I obeyed my mother, and I would have obeyed a husband after that. Here, I obey the mother prioress and our convent rules. We have a rule for everything, from the hour we get up, to the food we eat, the clothes we wear, the work we do. A rule for every hour of every day, every line of every prayer. But I know what the rules are, and they don't change if somebody drank too much wine."

"And one rule is that you can never leave the convent?"

"We leave the convent to come here. Where else would I go? Our convent is God's house. The Convent of the Santissima Annunziata. We call it the *bell' Nunnziatella.* We have a courtyard, a garden, a chapel, a kitchen. After you are baptized, you can live with us. You may not be happy, but you will be useful. You can read Latin already. I know you can, and I know you can sew. You will be busy. You will be safe.

"Perhaps you will not like us. We are ordinary women who were once very poor Jews and have become less poor Catholics. We do not have your education, but we have peace. We have the privacy of our thoughts and the comfort of our sisters. We are allowed nothing to read but the Gospels. But we are warm and fed, and if we are diligent in our duties, we are left alone."

She moves towards the bed where Anna is sitting and bends over her, lips pursing as she whispers.

"*Sh'ma*, Channà del Monte, don't think of your fancy family in the ghetto. It only makes you miserable. Build a cell in your mind, a calm place inside yourself where nothing can touch you. I made a cell in my mind and locked myself inside it. Make your own safe place. Never leave it. I pray you will find peace. I pray Christ will lift your sorrow."

And Anna thinks she will die there, sitting on that hard bed in that barren cell, imagining herself in a long black veil, locked away forever, never to see her home, her haven, never to feel Mammà's arms around her, Tatà's hand on her head. She wonders if she has asked Sister Innocènza the wrong questions, if God, her God, the God of Abraham will ask her something very different on the day of judgement.

HER NAME was Olimpia. That was the name her mother gave her, her Roman name. The rabbi called her Rivka, her Hebrew name. Her father sold old clothes and shoes, and sometimes he sold spoons and forks and slightly chipped dishes. He sold whatever he could find.

When someone dies in a hospital, their clothes, their shoes, the belongings they leave behind, are put away to be disposed of later. Twice a year, everything is bundled up, weighed, and sold by the kilo to the Jews. Olimpia's father was not a lazy man. On the morning of the sale, he was the first to roll his cart out the ghetto gate and over the Quattro Capi bridge to the Fatebenefrattelli hospital on the Tiberina Island. The friar who greeted him there was always an old man, because the younger monks are not permitted to speak to Jews for fear they might be contaminated. The friars of Fatebenefratelli are good souls. They send bandages and medicines to the ghetto, but a Jew is never permitted to enter their hospital. The punishment for a Jew who enters a Catholic hospital, monastery, convent, or oratory is three public lashings and a fine of twenty scudi—more money than Olympia's father had seen in his life.

The bundles were sold by weight. Olimpia's father had no idea what he was buying. He wheeled the bundles back to the ghetto where Olimpia, her mother and sister laboriously tore them apart, sorted the shoes from the gloves, the jackets from the breeches, the garments that could be salvaged from those that could not. For months afterward, Olimpia's father walked about the market at Piazza Navona and up and down the Via del

Corso shouting, "*Robbivécchi!*" Old stuff for sale! Or singing out "*Stracci, stracci, chi à scarpacce!*" Rags, rags! Who has shoes? Those with no money for shoes wrapped their feet in rags. Sometimes he practiced his sales cries at home to make his daughters laugh. It was Olimpia's happiest memory, that laughter. Perhaps it was her only happy memory.

The family lived in a single room on the Strada della Fiumara. Thanks be to God, it was three flights up, a *mazzàlle*, a stroke of luck. When the winter rains drenched Rome and the Tiber flooded the ghetto, their neighbors on the lower floors crowded in with them for weeks until the water receded, and the putrid mud could be removed. At times, three families lived in their room, which was barely large enough to accommodate a table and a bed. They had no kitchen, no toilet, no bath. They carried clean water from the fountain in the Piazza delle Tre Cannelle. The Tiber was closer, but the river was used for washing, defecating and fishing—not for cooking or drinking.

When Olimpia was twelve, she spent the day with her mother on the Vicolo della Torre, selling odd buttons and bits of ribbon from her father's bundles. As the sun began to set, her mother gave her a few coins to buy bread and goose fat for the evening meal. She raced back to their room with her little bundle, hungry, eager for her supper. But when she opened the door, she found her father dead on the bed, her mother weeping on the floor beside him. She never knew why he died. Her mother said he had used up everything he had been born with, and that was the end of him.

When Olimpia was sixteen, her sister, Desiderata,

whom the rabbi called Léa, married a man who made deliveries for the merchants on the Strada della Rua. He earned very little, but he was recently orphaned and had a room to himself, a place to bring a wife, a great luxury. Now it was Olimpia's turn to be gone, to give her mother a little peace in what was left of her life. The proposed husband was a widower with three children, nearly as old as her father would have been and in more or less the same line of work. She would have preferred to marry his oldest son, who was closer to her own age, but no one gave her a choice. The day the betrothal contract was to be signed, Olimpia told her mother she was going to the fountain, carried their clay jug down to the street, left it on the ground, and walked through the Pescaria Gate. She was very sorry to desert her mother, but the man's teeth were rotten, and his breath was so noxious that whenever he came near her, she thought she would vomit in his face.

She crossed Rome in terror, the yellow kerchief that marked her a Jew hidden in her skirt pocket, her eyes moving from side to side, on the lookout for sbirri. She was not at all clear where she was going, but for a young woman to appear lost or ask for directions would invite the worst kind of trouble. She climbed the steep Strada de' Serpenti to the Church of Santa Maria de' Monti, her eyes to the ground, praying no one would notice her. She recognized the Casa dei Catacumeni from a drawing she had seen of the frieze on the side of the building. Praying to the God of Abraham, the only god she knew, that no one would molest her, she rang the bell.

After a very long time, the grate opened, and a woman's eyes looked out at her. She took the yellow kerchief from her pocket and waved it. A jangling of keys, the noisy sliding of bolts. The Roman Olimpia, the Jewess Rivka, ceased to exist. When she took her vows, they gave her a Catholic name, Innocènza.

HANDS HIDDEN in the sleeves of her habit so that no part of her body can be seen, the prioress descends the slope of the Salita Del Grillo, clinging to the immense shadow of the Church of Saints Domenico and Sisto. The Novice Mistress, Sister Innocènza, walks beside her in pious silence, followed by a flutter of young women in white habits.

Only the prioress was born Catholic, and she regards her position as both a sacred duty and a punishment. She is a good and pious woman, but the dowry her family offered the Church was too small to buy her a more desirable situation. The rest of the flock were born in the ghetto, all of them converted and baptized, willingly or not. They are among the thirty sisters of the Santissima Annunziata, the only convent willing to accept converted Jews who might otherwise infect the purity of Catholic-born nuns. As they are already infected themselves, they serve the prioress and the rector at the contaminated Casa de Catacumeni, the House of Converts. Most of them came to the convent having been taught to pray in Hebrew and to read in Italian but little else. All of them were hopelessly poor, their convent dowries paid by noblewomen with good hearts and bad consciences.

The prioress, her wimpled head leaning to one side, whispers under her breath. "You were with the del Monte girl longer than usual this morning. One might hope she spoke to you. Did she not?"

"Yes, Mother Prioress, she asked how I came t' be a nun."

"Pronunciation, sister! Came *to* be a nun. I do wish you would enunciate properly."

The prioress is annoyed that Anna del Monte has spoken to Sister Innocènza when, despite all her efforts, she herself has been unable to elicit more than a few words from the girl. But she will never admit such prideful feelings, not even to herself. She whispers, "And you gave an appropriate response?"

"Yes, Mother. I shared my own gratitude."

The prioress hopes this is true. It is a risk to allow the Jewish inmates to speak to the converted nuns, but this del Monte has been impossibly obstinate. "I believe the girl has begun to soften," she says.

"Mother, you are a greater optimist than me."

"Than *I am*. You must learn to speak correctly, sister. No, I am not an optimist, but I am a believer. So long as we do God's work, our prayers will surely be answered. See that the opportunity arises to speak with this little Jewess again. Let her talk with you of whatever she likes. Show her that we are happy in the service of our Lord Jesus."

The prioress returns her gaze to the cobblestoned street, and Sister Innocènza knows that she is expected to perform the impossible.

~

THE PRIORESS has told Anna that Abbot Cavalli is so great a scholar that he has never honored such a one as she with his presence. She has been berated by a dozen priests, lectured by a curate and an archbishop. Now she is to be persuaded by a scholar. She hopes that this latest contender in the competition for her soul will be more interesting than the others.

The Abbot's eyes are so distorted by the thick lenses of his spectacles, she cannot be sure if he is looking at her, and he has a habit of gesturing with a long finger while pivoting in his chair as though he is trying to locate her.

"My dear little daughter," he says. They all begin this way, as if it will soften her heart to think of them as fathers. "I have come here to visit you, not of my own wish, but by order of His Holiness the Pope, so that I can have the honor of converting you by demonstrating points of your own laws, and by showing you the truth of our religion. I want to convince you with courtesy and pleasantness, so that you will hear me with every sweetness."

It is the pattern of her days to be fed honey in the morning and wormwood at night. She begins the day a strong and proud woman and ends it crouching on the floor like an animal.

"You know well," he says, "that the first thing you must do in the morning, immediately after washing your hands and face, is to say the *Shacharit, Baruch Asher Yatzar,* praying to the Divine to remove you from the temptations of the devil and to purify you."

She understands that they have sent another convert, a Jew with a circumcised *picciurèllo* in his breeches and a crucifix on his chest who means to drag her into Catholicism by instructing her in her own religion. He is a thin man with the spindly legs of a bird, modestly dressed in a black cassock, and he expects her to believe that he has come to help her.

The Signore Abbot's eyes are enormous behind his spectacles. He is indeed a formidable scholar who has prepared dozens of examples to support his premise that the truth of baptism and the coming of the messiah can be found in the Torah, the twenty-four books of the Hebrew bible. Catholicism, in his estimation, is simply the logical successor to Judaism and with one or two exceptions, the differences between the two religions are insignificant.

Anna thinks this is a disingenuous premise. If it is true, then why is it that for centuries, these negligible differences have been enough to cause kings and popes to oppress the Jews in ever more terrible ways?

This great scholar has been "helping" her for so long, her limbs are numb from sitting and her ears are sore from the monotony of his voice. At last, the vesper bells ring, reminding the Abbot that it is time to sum up his argument. He tells her that if she will only concede his very clear and simple points, she will gain the protection of God and of the saintly pope.

"And with that I will leave you happily," he says, "knowing that you will be convinced, since the pope himself has ordered that you must stay here for the entire quarantine of forty days. And if, by some chance, you should persist in your obstinacy, the prioress has only to say the word and a courier will be sent to the pope who will see that you are converted by force, if not by your own free will."

So, if reason fails, force will be applied. She says nothing. She only wants him to leave her in peace, but she would like to know why, if it is so simple to make a Christian of a Jew, he does not force her now? Why not rain holy water over the entire ghetto? Horace wrote, "*Vis consili expert mole ruit sua.*" Force without wisdom falls of its own weight. Let them force her. Let them fall.

WHILE THE nuns are walking back to the Convent of the Santissima Annunziata and Abbot Cavalli is lecturing Anna del Monte, the Marchesa Ludovica Falconieri-Albertoni is peering out the window of her carriage. She has instructed her coachman to drive her to the Church of Santa Maria in Campitelli and to leave her there. No one will find it strange that she has chosen to pray at the church of her father's family, nor will her decision to return home on foot be questioned. It is a fine day, after all, and she has brought her maid along. She crosses herself as she enters the church, then looks about. There should be a priest somewhere, a nun, perhaps an old beadle sweeping the aisles—anyone who will recognize her in the unlikely event that she needs a witness. Her maid has vouched for her before, but if the girl were threatened, she might become too frightened to be useful.

Light from the oculus in the enormous dome showers the marble floor of the nave, but the marchesa keeps to the shadows of a side aisle. She hurries to the Albertoni chapel, opens the gate, and enters, leaving her maid to wait. Busts of her ancestors peer out at her from the chapel walls, but the Marchesa sees only the frieze in front of her, which depicts the Holy Family as they appeared to the Blessed Ludovica Albertoni for whom she was named. When she was small, she often compared herself to this woman who was so pure of soul she experienced the ecstasy granted only to the most deeply religious. The marchesa had thought that she would follow this path, that she, too, would join the third order of Saint Francis and lead a selfless life, forsaking her wealth to administer to the sick and the poor. But then her breasts began to swell, hair sprouted between her legs, and she was sent home from the convent where she had been raised. At the Palazzo Albertoni, she was dressed in silk gowns. Her bosoms were decked with necklaces and her hair was perfumed. She began to notice that the eyes of the young men she met seemed to follow her, and she wondered what caused their britches to bulge.

ON THE other side of the ghetto wall, no more than a few hundred steps from the Church of Santa Maria in Campitelli, Rachele del Monte sits in the shadow of Buonafortuna Sermoneta's green grocery. A tribe of goats is milling around her feet, nosing the ground for bits of garbage, bleating joyfully at the discovery of a discarded apple core, the skin of an orange. Rachele's eyes are focused on her knitting, as though her fingers have forgotten the stitches they have made a thousand times, and she has to watch them to be sure they move correctly. Behind her, she hears the voice of the marchesa complaining as she picks her way through the garbage and goat dung. But Rachele looks up only when the toes of impeccable calfskin boots nearly touch her own sturdy shoes. She offers no greeting but silently appraises the young woman's red velvet cloak, the heavy satin of the skirt that rustles beneath it. Then, as though she has seen enough, Rachele lowers her eyes and returns to her knitting. She is taking a great risk, a Jewess who dares to humiliate an aristocrat.

The marchesa is vexed, but too proud to say so. She motions impatiently to her maid, who approaches Rachele with an outstretched hand, expecting her to reach under her apron and produce a vial of amber liquid. This afternoon, the old woman seems to have forgotten her role in the transaction. She ignores the maid and begins to knit another row. The potion the marchesa is so eager to obtain is a secret brew of giant fennel from Sardinia, blue cohosh root from the Americas, Egyptian wormwood, and the seeds of Queen Anne's lace. What the marchesa uses it for is a secret of another sort.

Rachele says it so quietly she might have been talking to herself. "I know the bed in which you will soon be lying." The marchesa bends down to the old woman in order to be sure she has heard correctly. "I know for whom you risk your reputation, whose child you must never carry. For how long have you enjoyed yourself without ever once conceiving? I have helped you many times. Now you will do something for me. And when you have done it, I will gladly sell you all the potions in the world."

Rachele looks up now to meet eyes that flash beneath a sheer black veil. They are deadlocked. If it becomes known that she buys potions in the ghetto, the marchesa will be shamed. A lesser woman might be excommunicated. But if the marchesa should turn on the old Jewess, no one would doubt her. Rachele would be arrested, even executed, burned at the stake. Without the old Jewess, the marchesa would have to find another source for the contraceptive potion she has come here to fetch. It would be difficult, perhaps impossible, and she would risk exposing herself to scandal. Rachele's potions have been reliable. They have never failed in their purpose or made her ill.

The marchesa's perfume is too heavy for Rachele's taste. These Catholic women wash infrequently and cover their bodily odors with scented French oils. She turns her head away as the marchesa breathes into her ear.

"Rachele, have pity on me. If you know who my husband is, you know that he is older than my father and that I never chose to marry him. But you do not know that in the privacy of our bedroom he rouges his cheeks and lips and draws his eyebrows with charcoal. You do not know what he wants me to do there, what I have had to do. Unnatural acts that could never result in a child."

Rachele's wooden needles click faster.

"Grandmother, perhaps it is true that you know the man for whom I buy your potions. But you do not know that he never chose a life of celibacy, that like me, his father chose for him. You do not know that we are able to steal only a few moments of happiness together, and that the price we will pay if we are discovered will be catastrophic."

Rachele puts down her knitting. "Fijema, I am sure you know that my granddaughter has been stolen from her family at gunpoint. She is young, with dreams and desires not so different from your own. Perhaps you know where they have taken her, but neither you nor I know what it is they do to her there or if she will ever be released. A word from you to this man with whom you share your secret pleasures, a tear or two wetting your cheek at the right moment could return her to her family. Go now. Do not let me see you again until I have seen my granddaughter, my Channà. When you have done as I ask, and Anna del Monte is released, you will send your maid to Angelo Zevi's shop. Instruct her to request a carved ivory comb for her mistress and I will hear of it. Zevi knows that I have such an item. He will ask me if I care to sell it. And when your maid comes to fetch the comb, she will find that I have placed something extra in the box."

THREE FRIARS have awoken Anna in her cell, bringing misery and noise. She is too tired to speak, too tired to move. How many hours has she spent like this, in this place, on this bed, silently listening, not listening? At least the one who speaks is young. His cassock is clean, his cheeks shaven, his skin clear. His features are fine, his eyes kind.

He says the same things she has heard again and again, asks the same questions she has already refused to answer. But he asks them gently, and when he looks at her, something in his face causes her to smile.

Why do they continue preaching and asking? "Do you believe in the Prophesies? Do you believe in the God of Israel? In the God of Abraham?" She has ignored these questions a hundred times before, yet when the young priest asks them, his silky voice spins a web. She likes watching his mouth as he speaks, watching the tip of his pink tongue wet his full lower lip. His body is slim and strong under his white tunic, his shoulders square, his back straight, and his fingers are long and pale, his nails clean.

She thinks he is beautiful, that the other priests have all been phantoms, and that this one is a man. Then she reminds herself that he is like all the others who entice her to answer them, to say something they can grasp, a straw they can hold up and claim that she has been converted, that she has, at last, seen the light they have all been trying so hard to show her. How proud this young man would be to succeed when so many others have failed! He asks again, and again, and again, and she remains mute, silently watching him.

They talk to her day and night, hour after hour. If she says nothing, this one will remain here until he has devoured her and then another, even hungrier priest will be sent in.

He asks very softly, pleadingly. "Surely, you believe in the God of Moses. In the God of David? The God of Solomon?" His voice is like music played somewhere far away. She is closer to sleep now than waking. She closes her eyes, burrows through the mist in her head to the Strada della Rua. Tatà takes her hand, leading her through the dusk. Where are we going? It doesn't matter, my Channà.

"Anna, Anna, do you hear me?" A sweet, tender sound, soft breath caresses her ear.

"Do you believe in the god of your forefathers and mine?"

How can she deny that she believes in her own god? It's too absurd. She murmurs, "*Certo, ci credo.*" Of course, I believe it.

And the wolves are howling, baring their teeth. The friars are raising their arms in triumph, praising their savior, their *mumzer*. The young one silences them. "Quiet, all of you! She has said the words and it is done."

It is done! What poisonous words has she said? "*Certo, ci credo.*" What can that mean to them? She has admitted nothing, promised nothing. Still her enemies declare victory and she is trapped forever in their midst. She has betrayed her family, deprived them of the joy of her sister's wedding. Her father, her mother will never smile again.

How can she take a single breath, live a single minute longer? The rector will find a Christian husband for her, an ignorant *goi* with a *chiuso* between his legs. And if she refuses to marry, the prioress will force her to join Christ's harem. She will spend all the days of her life smothered in a nun's habit, a wimple crushing her head. She would rather be locked in this cell until her eyes fall out, her skin turns to dust and her bones crumble.

The friars are on their knees, hands clasped, faces lifted to the ceiling, giving thanks to their savior for allowing them to subdue the obstinate Jewess.

Qowli el elohim weha azin. I cry aloud to God that He may hear me. In the day of my trouble, I seek the Lord. My hand is stretched out in the night and does not rest. My soul refuses to be comforted.

She is too weak to speak, but she can scream. "Do you think you have convinced me because I finally answered you after hours of interrogation? Do you think you have snared me, pulled me away from my own sacred religion? I am stronger in my faith now than ever before. Do not think you can suffocate me with your falsehoods, because no one can force me to say what I do not believe. I am neither frightened by your extravagant threats nor impressed by your ridiculous propositions. I only want to return to my home. I have said this since the day I was brought here. Do not tell me that it is done. You make me laugh! I was born a Jew and I will die a Jew. Vicegerent de' Rossi never authorized you to behave so shamefully, nor would he allow you to force anyone to give up her soul, even if you think you do it with good intentions."

The friar begins to circle the little cell, around and around, staring at the ceiling, his lips moving. When he stops, it is as though his god has answered him. "You are such an intelligent woman," he says in the imploring tone of a suitor, "such a strong woman. It will be my great honor to convert you. The vicegerent himself has informed me of his great respect for your family."

Anna does not believe the vicegerent even knows this friar's name. The priests, still on their knees, look at her silently for a moment. The young one is staring at her, not at her face, but at her body, his face filled with horror. Her shawl has come away from her shoulders, exposing her collar bone. She covers herself quickly with one hand while pulling her shawl close with the other. Then she wraps herself in the blanket and moves away from him, her back against the wall.

The friar has begun to stamp about like a demon, his body shaking, his fine features contorted. She crouches on the bed, cringing, dreading what he will do. He is untying the rope from his waist. Does he mean to undress in front of her? He is fashioning a big knot from one end of the rope. Now he holds it by the other end and raises it over his head. Does he mean to flog her? She cannot bear to watch him. His face has a look of such agony, such desperation, she could weep for him.

Badonai! He is thrashing himself, snapping the knotted end of the rope against his own flesh. Each time he raises the rope over his head he groans, and as he strikes, he cries out in the grip of a passion she has never seen and has no wish to understand.

The other friars are on their feet, pulling at his arms, dragging him to the door.

Sparks fly through Anna's body. Her breath is as rapid as if she had been running. A fire rages between her legs, her thighs are damp. She screams, "Stop! Stop! Stop!"

The friar turns to look at her with crazed eyes, the rope limp in his hands. And she is ashamed that it has given her pleasure to drive him mad.

THEY HAVE left her. She is on the floor, hugging her knees. She crawls into her thoughts, into a billowing tent, where she is safe. She is in the women's gallery at the kal, sitting beside her sister. The cantor stands on his platform singing, his voice full of sorrow. A blue-striped shawl covers his shoulders, and his head is crowned with a tall white hat. Through the grates she can see Gabriele Sereni, her beautiful young man, a skullcap topping his dark curls, holding his prayer book in soft white hands. Will he be sad if she disappears forever, devoured by lions?

Has he asked Tranquillo what has happened to her? Does he think of her in his sleeplessness as she thinks of him? She is eighteen years old. After her sister's wedding, it will be her turn to collect pretty things for her trousseau, her dònora, her turn to be the challà, the bride.

Ascem, Ascemme, Amènne Amènne, coi nome di Dio sia semipro Amènne, Mammà's lullaby. She sings herself to sleep.

TRANQUILLO DEL Monte carefully negotiates the narrow Vicolo Del Capocciuto, his fingertips tracing the wall to his right. There are no street lamps, no sentries bearing torches, and not wishing to be noticed, he carries no light with him. He finds his way in the dimness of a moon nearly obliterated by tall buildings on either side of the alley. His eyes scan the ground, trying to avoid tripping over one of the holes that pit the street or stepping into filth. He walks slowly, feeling the uneven cobblestones beneath his feet, the dirt and trash and gravel. Dozens of souls lurk behind each wall, but the streets are dark. Not a single window is fitted with glass, not a single candle flickers in any of them. With his fingertips, he finds a doorway, a lintel. There are no street signs, no house numbers.

Tranquillo's father, Benedetto del Monte, is a member of the Congregation of Sixty, which administers life in the ghetto. His uncle, Angelo Zevi, is one of the three memunim, the elected governors. They will do everything they can imagine to free Anna, but their imaginations are limited by the laws. The Catholic laws. A Jew may petition the Tribunal of the Inquisition. A Jew may write pleadingly to the vicegerent, to the civil lieutenant prelate, to the cardinal vicar, even to the pope himself. Sometimes this has a good effect. More often it has no effect at all. Despite all their efforts, Devora Panzieri was never heard from again. The children of Davide Sermoneta vanished. Tranquillo can think of a dozen, two dozen stories without stretching his memory very far into the past. This cannot, must not happen to his sister, his Channà. He will not let it happen.

He is young, too young to comprehend the impotence of the Jews. Even when he becomes old enough to understand it, he will refuse to accept it as his father and his uncle have done. At the age of twenty-six, he is still certain that he can change the order of things. He refuses to believe he lacks the resources to arrange his sister's release. After all, he has connections. He knows certain gentiles who know certain gentiles. And he has important friends in the ghetto.

Tranquillo is a good-looking man. His auburn hair is silky, his complexion unblemished. His light brown eyes are bright, and he has a way of using them to enchant people, gazing intently from under heavy lids, his chin lowered, so that he seems to be searching for the essence of those who speak to him, smiling slightly as though every word they utter fascinates him. Outside his family, he is considered irresistible. Family members pretend to be immune to his charms. In his presence, they tolerate him. In his absence, they adore him.

The meeting is in a room six steps down from the street where Gabriele Sereni's father stores goods for his hardware shop. The dim and musty space might house an extended family of six or eight, but the Sereni are prosperous by ghetto standards and can afford to use the room for storage. When Tranquillo enters, he finds wooden crates and rough cloth sacks stacked to the ceiling. Odd items are scattered here and there—a box of old nails, iron hooks, a mallet.

The men arrive one by one to avoid attracting attention—Abramo Finzi, Solomone Ambron, Raffaele Vito and Allegrezza's betrothed, Crescenzio Castelnuovo. They squeeze their legs through the spaces between crates, climb over stacks of goods, find spots to sit on. A single oil lamp is kept low and placed in the back of the room so that no passerby will suspect that anyone is inside.

Tranquillo is not sure what his friends can accomplish here, but it is better to do something, anything. Better, at least, to talk as though something can be done. Each man knows someone who might know someone—a nobleman, a churchman who might trade his influence for a favor.

These young Jews can arrange illicit loans, a room where a gentile can spend a discrete hour. They can provide that most exotic of delicacies, a Jewess, a woman whom Voltaire called "a splendid reproduction of her mother Eve." A velvet-eyed widow with alabaster skin, a voluptuous daughter of Abraham with a useless husband and children to feed, a woman who cannot afford to be fussy about her honor. A night, even an hour, with a Jewess is the ultimate pleasure because the punishment for it is death. Canon law proscribes sexual relations between Jews and gentiles. Only men who have connections at the Inquisition can afford such a luxury, men who know whom they must bribe.

A jug of wine is passed across sacks and boxes. Earthenware cups are filled and refilled. Tranquillo has listened to idea after idea, but there has been too much chatter, and nothing has been decided. "So," he says as loudly as he dares. "Now we must make a plan of action. Solomone, your father is physician to Count Orsini. You have promised to do what you can. If the old count is feeling better, he will be in a mood to reward your father. Perhaps he can be persuaded to write a few words on Anna's behalf. Crescenzio, you have a friend who is a clerk at the Tribunal. You must ask him to pass a message to Cardinal Ruffo, but we must be very careful what it says. We will write it together in a manner that is inarguably persuasive while maintaining the greatest humility.

"Abramo, did you tell me that you sold a Turkish carpet to the pope's secretary of state? What is his name? Gonzaga, yes. He is a great collector of fine things. Perhaps he has already done business with my father or my uncle. A man whose heart is touched by artistry will see an advantage in freeing the daughter of an antiques dealer. Baruccabbà! Here is Giacomo."

Devora Panzieri's brother Giacomo arrives late. He is the least optimistic of the men, but they defer to him because he alone has done this before. He has tried— and failed—to free his sister from the Catacumeni where Anna del Monte has just awoken from a nightmare.

SHE WAS coughing, choking, unable to breathe. The cell

was filled with smoke, swirling in the dark. Blindly stumbling, she ran to the door but there was no door. She ran to the window, but there was no window. Thick stone walls surrounded her, crushed her. She waved her arms frantically, uselessly trying to fan the smoke away. Her eyes burned. Her forehead throbbed. She thought this must be hell, the inferno, that the goim had been right, that she had been condemned to eternal suffering.

Then she knew it was a dream, a nightmare. And now she is gasping, her body curled tightly against itself, her eyes open. Too terrified to sleep.

The restrictions of the popes, the papal bulls and missives, are posted on the ghetto gates, at the Campo de' Fiori, the Piazza Navona, at the fish market and along the bridges that cross the Tiber—all the places where they will be seen by Jews who will shudder and weep, and by Catholics who will laugh, or sneer, or shake their heads in pity. One by one, decade after decade, pope after pope has restricted and tormented the obstinate Jews who could be free of all these constraints if only they would have the good sense to convert.

Jews May Not:
◊ Reside outside the ghetto walls or in villas, farms, villages, or other occupancies under any pretext whatever.
◊ Keep shops, warehouses, or stables outside the ghetto walls.
◊ Be seen outside the ghetto without identifying clothing, including a yellow hat or veil.

◊ Be seen outside the ghetto from one hour after dusk until one hour after dawn.

◊ Appear in public during Holy Week.

◊ Trade in new objects of any kind.

◊ Engage in business with a Christian.

◊ Sell Christian religious objects new or old.

◊ Sell meat to a Christian.

◊ Engage in banking or make loans.

◊ Practice medicine on Christians.

◊ Employ Christian servants.

◊ Own horses or carriages.

◊ Place a stone or any inscription whatever on the grave of a Jew.

◊ Use any rite, ceremony, or pomp in their funerals, and especially, they must refrain from singing psalms, carrying torches or lights through the streets.

◊ Keep in their possession, read, buy, write, copy, translate, sell, give, exchange, or in any other matter whatever under any pretext, title, or color, any book or impious manuscripts, whether Talmudic or containing any injurious impiety or blasphemies against the Holy Scriptures or the Old Testament, or against the Holy Mysteries of the Christian faith.

◊ Leave Rome for any reason other than to attend a fair, and only with a license *in scriptis* issued by a bishop, inquisitor, or local vicar. Such travel not to exceed three days after the fair has ended, four days in case of rain. Such license must be presented to the bishop, inquisitor, or local vicar at the location of the fair immediately upon arrival.

◊ Keep in his house a neophyte or catechumen of either sex, much less eat, drink, or sleep with one, either in or outside the ghetto or in any other place, work with them, or converse with them even by letter, and even if they are related by the first degree of sanguinity, be they father, mother, son, daughter, brother, sister, or other relation.

◊ Approach within the space of sixty yards the Casa dei Catacumeni or the Convent of the Santissima Annuziata in Rome.

◊ Dissuade neophytes or converts from embracing the True Faith, or in any way attempt to persuade them to leave the Good Road.

◊ Hide or in any way aid a Jew who has been offered to the Church.

Punishments May Include:

Fines of any amount, public lashings, imprisonment, banishment, execution.

H OW MANY more mornings will she awaken to the dim light of this tiny, barred window, these streaked white walls, the smell of dry straw and stone, whispers in the corridor, the clanging of keys? It is all she can do to force herself to say the morning prayers, to wash, to dress. She is beyond caring whether she eats or starves, wakes or sleeps, lives or dies, but she will never imprison her heart and her mind as Sister Innocènza has done.

She has decided to comfort herself each morning with a story to prevent her memories from being buried in the avalanche of Catholic preaching that thunders over her hour after hour, day after day. While the newborn sun is still too weak to reach this dark cell, she sits up in bed and tries to remember a particular *Succot*.

She was four years old, too young to be much help, but old enough to be thrilled as she sat with her sister on the threshold of the shop, watching their father, grandfather, and brother assemble the family *succa* commemorating the huts their ancestors built in the fields during the harvest. She tried to imagine Jews who lived in the countryside and worked the land. But those ideas were too far from her reality, too far from her life in the ghetto. Succot is the best holiday of the year, the only one without reference to something bad—being enslaved in Egypt or being persecuted by a wicked tax collector or atoning for sins.

And now she is four years old again, watching the men set up planks of scrap wood to form a frame, creating walls and a ceiling from the palm fronds and leafy branches the wind blew onto the streets. In her eyes, these men are giants, magicians who talk and laugh while they work, as though building a house from nothing is the easiest job in the world.

Mammà and Savta Rachele are both beautiful women, even when clothed as they are in their oldest dresses, their hair covered with kerchiefs. She watches them sweep the cobblestones, then layer threadbare rugs to make a floor. Anna and Allegrezza are allowed to help them hang plants in each corner of the hut, decorate the ceiling and walls with grapevines and pomegranates, bits of colored ribbon and paper garlands.

When the hut is complete, the little girls, nearly exploding with excitement, sing and dance, hold hands and whirl around until they are so dizzy, they fall onto the old carpets, and Anna lies on her back looking up at the ceiling, watching the palm fronds shatter the sunlight.

In her memory, theirs was the most wonderful hut in the ghetto. She runs up and down the Strada della Rua, clutching Allegrezza's hand, peeking into all the other huts, laughing. Devora's family has decorated their hut with strips of brightly colored fabric. Chiara's family hut is filled with flowering cyclamen. But the del Monte hut is the best, the prettiest. She is four years old, and still believes that everything her family does, everything they have, is the best in the world. It will be years before she realizes that they are only a little more fortunate than the other poor Jews, all of them confined to the ghetto.

As is the custom, they eat their evening meal in the hut, sitting cross-legged on the old rugs. Tatà laughs with Dod Angelo. Tranquillo plays with Ester's hair. Mammà sits in a corner talking softly with Dod Angelo's wife, Doda Sara. And when Anna tries to sit on Mammà's lap, she tells her to go play with Ester and Allegrezza.

It is early fall, and the sun sets slowly. One by one, the lamps are lit, and the streets fill with goim who come every year to see the decorated huts, ignoring their pope's interdiction. Mammà stands at the entrance to their succa, watching the crowds, her hand caressing Anna's head. If someone stops to admire their hut, Anna has been told to say *"baruccabbà,"* welcome," and offer a *ginetti* cookie. She is a tiny, gracious hostess, holding a plate of cookies, smiling, "baruccabbà."

A little Christian girl lags behind her parents, chewing her cookie, staring. All Anna's playmates are as Jewish as she is. She thinks that goim should look different somehow. She should be able to tell who is Jewish and who is not. But this little girl could have been her sister. She has the same green eyes, the same auburn curls, the same cotton dress. Anna takes the girl by the hand so that she can have a better peek inside. "Look," she says. "Look how pretty our *succa*."

In the desolation of her cell, Anna thinks that remembering may be a bad idea, that there is no greater sorrow than to recall happiness in times of misery. Outside this Catholic prison, it is spring. Summer will come, then Rosh haShana, Iom Kippur, and on the fifteenth day of the month of Tishrei, the del Monte family will make a succot again. By then, Allegrezza will be married. And Anna? Where will she be?

Two years earlier

Pope **BENEDICT XIV**
TO
Ferdinando maria de' Rossi, *by the grace of God, and of
the Apostolic Holy See, Archbishop of Tarso and Vicegerent
of the City*
February 28, 1747

Venerable Brother, Greetings and Apostolic Benedictions
*From reading Genesis Chapter 3, the Jews are well
aware that the wife is under the control of the husband. They
cannot deny that, even according to their own custom, to be
betrothed permits the future husband a certain right, a certain authority over his future bride and perhaps even more
than that which a Christian acquires over his future wife.*
*Neither can the Jews complain of the offering of the wife
and of the betrothed woman, who is carried off to spend
forty days at the Casa dei Catacumeni no sooner than her
spouse or betrothed converts, or expresses a wish to convert,
and offers her to the Church. The man is always taken at his
word without the necessity of proof that a betrothal contract,
valid according to their custom, has been executed. And this
has caused a great deal of lamentation among the Jews who*

claim some sort of invalidity and will say that it is not the first time that such a rank and cowardly lover, desperate because he has been refused the hand of the woman within the confines of his own religion, resorts to this path, falsely claiming to be betrothed.

Since 1725, it has been recognized that once a Jew has repented of his false beliefs and offers his future bride to the Church, she is to be taken forthwith to the Casa dei Catacumeni and restrained there for forty days. And so, it becomes a matter of determining the legitimacy of the claim of betrothal, and this cannot be our concern. If the claim has no other basis than the word of the repentant Jew, the strength of the promise is as valid as the betrothal contract.

In the case of the Hebrew fiancé who converts to the Christian faith, and makes an offer of the fiancée, it will be your task to interrogate her, or to cause her to be interrogated, in order to ascertain the verity of the supposed betrothal, without being obliged to believe a single assertion. During the process, it will also be your task to recognize, or have recognized, the validity of the betrothal as it is recognized between Christians, requiring only the testimony of witnesses or a valid conjecture.

She should be sent to the Casa dei Catacumeni for forty days, only if she were to display some reasonable hope of conversion. If, however, she remains obstinate in her perdition, she must be sent back to the ghetto.

THIS MORNING, for the first time, the nun in the black veil has brought Anna her boiled egg, a jug of water and a bit of bread. Anna has no friends in this place, but this nun, this Sister Innocènza, as she is called, is at least a familiar face. She does not leave the food on the table and rush off, like the white nuns who come to her every day, eyes on their feet, as though the sight of another Jew is so dangerous, they dare not look at her.

Sister Innocènza stands with her hands hidden in the sleeves of her habit and looks at Anna fearlessly, even kindly. "The vicegerent will be here today," she says. "He'll be back t' talk t'you."

Anna is seated on the hard bed, her hands in her lap, her chin on her chest, too tired to raise her head. How will she survive another day of this, another endless lecture, another night invaded by rabid priests, threatening her with their holy water? And now the vicegerent. What more can he want of her?

"The prioress will take you from this cell to the *parlatorio*. It's beautiful, with paintings and cushioned couches. You'll see."

Anna doesn't raise her head, but her eyes are open wide and her hands are damp. To leave this cell. To meet the vicegerent. Perhaps today she will be free. The memunim have succeeded. The Christian lawyer has persuaded the Inquisition. Someone has accepted a bribe ... something. Why else would the vicegerent come to this place? Why else would the prioress lead her from this cell?

"You should be ready for him," the nun says. "You should fix your hair. Tie your bodice proper."

Anna looks up to watch the nun pull a wooden comb from the folds of her habit. And she smiles, lifts her head and squeezes shut her damp, red eyes.

When the nun leaves, Anna's hair is neatly twisted on top of her head, held by her silver pin. Her bodice is properly tied, her scarf arranged to cover her collarbone, she paces the cell, then stands at the window, clutching the bars. She bites her lips till they bleed, then worries that she won't look well when her family sees her. A dozen times, she brushes her wrinkled skirt with the back of her hand, folds back her sleeves to hide the stains. Folds and refolds. And she waits, waits, waits, resists tearing at her hair, scratching at her cheeks. She tries to stay neat. She smiles, laughs out loud. It is over, surely it is over. She counts the bits of eggshell hidden at the back of her food box, and half an hour later, she counts them again.

She hears the rattle of keys, the lock turning, and she jumps in the air, raising her arms. But it is only the black-veiled nun again, bringing her more bread, more water, a bowl of strange soup she dares not eat. Who knows what tarèffe might be in it.

"Anna del Monte," the nun says, "after you have eaten and rested, the prioress will come for you, Be ready."

Anna looks at her, eyes wild, and says nothing. She will soon be gone from here. She has no need of this Jewish nun.

She has no need of this *goishe* soup. Her mother will have roasted a capon. Her grandmother will have fried artichokes. The bread will be laced with raisins and almonds.

She sits on the bed, pulls her knees to her chest, and thinks of the joy in her father's face when he sees her, feels her mother's arms crushing her. She feels the softness of Savta Rachele's breast. Soon she will lay her head there. She thinks of her sister Allegrezza, of handsome Gabriele Sereni at the kal in his kippah and tallis.

When she hears the door groan on its hinges, the cell

is already cloaked in dusk. The prioress stands before her, shaking her head, clapping her hands. "Come now, my child. Hurry, the vicegerent is waiting."

She takes Anna's arm, and leads her through the open door, down a stone staircase, along a corridor. With every step, Anna's smile becomes broader, her heart beats faster. They are moving towards freedom. A carriage will be waiting to take her back to the ghetto, back to her home.

She can see the door that opens onto the street, locked and barred. But just as they reach it, the prioress squeezes her arm and pulls her around a corner into a large, cheerless room. A grill covers the windows, partitioning the light so that the stone floor is carpeted in intricate shadows. A painting over the hearth depicts their messiah bleeding on the cross against a black sky, surrounded by dead trees and buzzards. The ceiling is frescoed with images of women, each suffering great bodily anguish, each wearing an oddly serene expression, as though she is not at all bothered by being tied to a wheel, burned at the stake, beheaded by a sword. Anna can hear faint noises from the street outside, fragments of conversation, footsteps, hooves on cobblestones, and she tells herself that soon, she, too, will be in the open air, in the world, never to return to this dim and sorrowful place.

The Most Illustrious Vicegerent de' Rossi, in all his finery, has made himself comfortable on a well-cushioned divan. He does not stand when she appears but lifts a hand heavy with rings and motions for her to sit opposite him on an upholstered chair. The prioress bows, backs away, lurks in the corridor.

The vicegerent has come himself to tell her that she

will be returned to her family, that he has made a mistake. She is a del Monte, a Zevi, she should never have been brought here. Anna holds her head like a countess and greets him very gladly, as though she is delighted to see his bony face again. He must have received letters from her father, her Dod Angelo, Rabbi Mielì, and the Catholic attorney, Signor Battaglia. He must have realized that she was abducted falsely. Before she sits, she lowers her eyes and curtseys, smiling, murmuring, "Your Excellency, I am honored."

The vicegerent's mouth is full of honey. He asks if she has been treated well, and she feels the eyes of the prioress watching from the shadows. He wants to know if the great scholar he has sent for her conversion has had the desired effect, and she struggles to keep from weeping. He says his only purpose is to instruct her, so that she may leave the darkness of the Jewish religion and enter the light of the one true faith, lest her soul remain lost in the infernal abyss. Each word he speaks tears at her flesh. He has not come to release her, but to rebuke her.

"My daughter," he says, "think well on your situation. Know that what we do here is entirely for your benefit. Nothing matters to us but the salvation of your soul, and we are obliged to do everything possible to help you embrace the Catholic religion. Reflect on this. There is no recourse before the Tribunal of God. You have had the benefit of many hours of preaching. Many learned men have urged you to open your heart. If you cannot hear what we have tried so hard to teach you, you will never enjoy the presence of God. Think on this, my little daughter. The life of the world is but an instant, and though the glory of God's grace is eternal, it will be denied to those who refuse to enlist under the banner of Peter."

He sits with his hands clasped, dark little eyes flickering, and tells her the same things she has heard a thousand times since she was brought to this cruel place. "It is not true that we wish to convert you by force," he says. "Our dearest wish is that you will convert spontaneously and with a joyful heart. I pray to God that He may enlighten you. I did not expect to find you so obstinate, but I will pray for you. I promise to be your protector and to lead you with my own hands to the Sacred Font."

She imagines that he will honor her by sprinkling her head with his *madett'a* water. She will become Anna de' Rossi, the pious Catholic. No, that would be too grand. He will christen her simply Anna Rossi, to avoid polluting his noble family. And he will choose a decidedly Catholic name for her—Cristiana Rossi, perhaps.

The vicegerent is waiting for her response. What can she say to the man who means to steal her life? She fears him greatly, but she loathes him even more.

"*Illustre Signore*, I am imprisoned in this place innocently without knowing the cause. You have the power to order my death, however unjustly, but my soul belongs absolutely and only to my God, my Holy Law, and my honorable parents. This was my first response when I was brought here, and it will by last response, even if I say it with my dying breath."

He has risen from the divan and steps towards her, but she remains seated and will not look away. "You may sentence me to death or condemn me to a cloistered life among nuns, but I will still be a Jew."

"Hold your tongue!" His voice is like a knife. "As I find you so obdurate, be assured that you will receive full justice from me."

Anna looks away to find the prioress making the sign of the cross.

~

THE VICEGERENT'S stomach has woken him again tonight. It gives him trouble no matter how little he eats. He stands by his bedroom window peering out into the dark. Wearing only his nightshirt, a woolen shawl covering his shoulders, he watches as a man carrying a lantern up the wide slope of the Monte Citorio turns away discreetly to avoid illuminating the face of a passerby.

De' Rossi has several rooms in the Palazzo Della Ospizio Apostolico—reception rooms, a dining room, a library and study—but he has chosen the smallest of them as his bed chamber because it faces away from the busy Piazza della Colonna. Even so, he can hear the distant sound of a woman's laughter, the shouts of drunken men and the clatter of horses' hooves as a carriage rolls along the Via del Corso. He thinks perhaps he ought to pray, that his conscience bothers him more than his stomach, but he is too uncomfortable and weary even for prayer.

He spent the afternoon with Francesco Mileti, rector of the Casa dei Catacumeni, a man who rarely fails to upset his digestion. The house was established two centuries ago as a place for seclusion and introspection, a cloister where women who wished to convert to Catholicism could affirm their decision. The quarantine of forty days was only introduced for instruction in the faith before baptism. It was never meant to become an extended period of coercion.

Mileti knows that de' Rossi abhors forced baptism, but that never gives him pause because he also knows that the vicegerent answers to the pontiff, whose greatest wish is to convert every infidel on earth. This morning when he inquired why the del Monte girl was being held so long, Mileti replied that "Women have the genius to be obstinate for many, many days before they declare themselves, and so the forty-day quarantine is necessary." With a tight-lipped smile, he explained that the Jews ruin their daughters. "These young Jewesses have been too well educated. They read and write as well as a man, sign contracts, choose their own husbands and birth very few children. I suspect they use some witchcraft to avoid birthing more. The religion is passed down through the mother, which gives them the illusion of power. They say that they live to fulfill the wishes of their husbands, but they are insufficiently humble. Even when the husband sees the light of Christ, he cannot command his wife to join him in the arms of the Holy Church, and she must be taken by force."

De' Rossi chose not to waste time debating these points. Mileti, that vile worm, loves to boast of how well he tames the Jewesses who pass through his doors. "It is morally desirable to torture them for a few days until they accept Christ, and thereby save them from the eternal torments of hell," he said, fingering the cross on his breast. "Even the most ferocious lioness becomes a meek lamb in the fold of Jesus Christ, and at the moment of baptism, they lose that *foetor judaicus*, that unpleasant Jewish odor."

The purpose of de' Rossi's visit was not to endure the rector's opinions, but to further interview the del Monte girl, who remains intractable after a week of seclusion, despite the reasoned efforts of the greatest theologians in Rome and the spurious threats of the rector's most fanatic preachers, all of them converted Jews, desperate men from the most miserable ghetto streets who wheedle and maw to ensure their steady supply of bread and minestrone. The rector sends them into the cells two and three at a time, so that the least experienced can learn by observing the methods of the most successful. They are the *canes domini*, God's ravenous dogs, constantly experimenting, inventing more efficacious means of persuasion, vying to capture the greatest number of souls.

Anna del Monte is a prime specimen, an educated girl from an important family, a prize for the Church. That morning, de' Rossi had tried to be gentle with her, certain he could gain her trust. He released her from her cell, interviewed her in the comfort of the parlatorio with all the courtesy due a countess. But it was impossible to reason with this girl who is as stubbornly attached to her Hebrew beliefs as Miloti is to his bigotry. When he spoke of the salvation of her soul, she answered him so disdainfully he became exasperated. It galls him that an insolent eighteen-year-old Jewess could cause him to lose the composure he has managed to maintain in the face of tyrannical popes and kings.

De' Rossi puts a hand to his stomach, feels its contents roiling like *stufato* in a cauldron. The Jews have ruined his digestion. Perhaps he should pull the bell rope to ring for Claudio, his young valet, who is asleep in the dressing room just on the other side of the wall. The boy's face is pale and soft, his cheeks barely marred by the hint of an incipient beard. His buttocks are high and round, his calves plump and firm. De' Rossi thinks he might ring for the laudanum bottle, simply for the pleasure of admiring Claudio's delicious body. There was a time when a boy like that might have comforted him in his sleeplessness, but those days are all but gone.

He has little appetite even for the Marchesa Falconieri-Albertoni, who, at twenty-eight, is too young and lusty to be satisfied by a frail old cleric. In his weathered arms, she attempts to fulfill a fantasy she harbored as a girl at convent school when she saw no man but the priest who celebrated mass and heard her confession. He wonders that she still slips longing notes into prayer books passed to his valet by her maid. He knows it is whispered in the corridors of the Vatican that he shares his bed with a noblewoman, but few in the Church will fault him for that. Few can cast the first stone.

Five years before, he had been struck by the perfection of her pale breasts rising above a lace-trimmed bodice. When her ridiculous husband presented her to him, Ludovica curtsied and looked up with pleading eyes.

She has not asked for her usual "audience" this month. Instead, she has written that by releasing the del Monte girl, he will be releasing her, as well—a marchesa for the price of a Jewess. Another of Ludovica's riddles, hinting at something she cannot safely put on paper.

He has had too many unguarded moments with this woman, whose silky skin, soft flesh, and worshipful gaze trick him into believing that she is the one person on earth he can trust. The last time he saw Ludovica, her thick, dark hair drifted over his face, and in its shadow, he became the small boy who hid under the dining table, whispering to his cat, safe and adored, while the angry voices of the adults rose above him. Ludovica stroked his cheek and kissed his forehead, and he wanted to tell her that he wonders if he is the only prelate whose conscience is at odds with his ambition. Instead, he told her about Anna del Monte.

Women like Ludovica send their maids to the ghetto to buy beauty creams and potions from superstitious Jewish grandmothers. There must be talk there. The del Monte girl must be a cause célèbre.

De' Rossi feels with his hands in the dark for the arms of his chair, lowers himself onto it and pulls his shawl more tightly around his shoulders. In a few hours, he will be wigged and powdered, dressed in his finest silks, and driven to the Vatican to appear before the pope.

Benedict XIV is an intellectual, a philosopher who proudly calls the heretic Voltaire a friend. He nurtures his reputation as a kind-hearted pontiff, a man of the people who walks the streets of Rome like an ordinary citizen, stopping to talk with whomever he happens to meet, even in the rough Trastevere quarter where no other pope has deigned to tread. Perhaps Benedict is truly kind, even to the Jews, but he believes that it is his sacred mission to make every one of them a Christian, to remove at its roots every trace of Jewish religion and culture.

In the morning, de' Rossi will be the bearer of disappointing news. Twice weekly, the pope greets him hopefully, expecting a new victory, another conversion, another soul saved. Benedict has revoked the rights of Jewish parents so that any child above the age of seven can be baptized against their will. One parent can baptize a child without the consent of the other. If a grandfather offers a fatherless grandchild, it will be seized from its mother.

Jews can be taken to the Casa dei Catacumeni on the flimsiest of charges—a word overheard, a claim of kinship. De' Rossi is left to quell the protests after babies have been snatched, after young women like the del Montes' daughter have been torn from their families. And after the Church has stolen their children from them, he must meet with the memunim, the governors of the ghetto, to discuss terms for repayment of the Jews' enormous debt to the Holy Congregation.

De' Rossi knows the Jews better than anyone at the Vatican, but even he fails to fully comprehend them. The ruling class are educated men, thinking men, who speak flawless Italian and read Latin. They can tell a fine work of art from a forgery and play a more than decent game of Faraone. He finds it impossible to understand why they cling so tenuously to a religion that provides them with nothing but grief and degradation.

The Ambron and the del Monte had been among the wealthiest families in Rome before Innocent XI revoked Jewish banking licenses. Why hadn't they converted then to save their fortunes and the futures of their descendants? What madness compels them to cling to their faith, when only a few simple tenets separate Judaism from Christ?

For nearly two centuries, the Jews of Rome have been crowded into a pestilential enclosure in the lowest part of the city, their rights gradually but continuously diminished, and yet the Church has not converted a tenth of them. Every barrel of wine, every loaf of bread, every pinch of salt is taxed. The Jews are compelled to pay for the guards who patrol the ghetto gates, for the carnival games to which they are not invited. They are taxed six hundred scudi a year to maintain the Casa dei Catacumeni and an additional three hundred to maintain the Convent of the Santissima Annuziata for the converted. They must pay the parishes for the sermons they are forced to attend on Saturday afternoons. They must even pay a yearly stipend of thirty-six scudi to the vicegerent himself. The Jewish debt to the papal treasury has risen to 280,000 scudi, most of it unpaid interest—a figure four times greater than the combined worth of them all.

Again tomorrow, the pope, wearing his most benign smile, will ask, "Doesn't the Church triumph more fully over the Jews in convincing and converting them than if once and for all she destroyed them with the edge of the sword?" The pope will say again that "the Church has infinite patience." But it must be clear, even to him, that this method of conversion through hardship has failed.

At times de' Rossi wonders if he should pray for the courage to say so, but the thought always passes. Such brash words would only result in his own fall from grace, and nothing would change for the Jews. A few of them convert every year, some willingly, more under duress. Mothers convert to join the children who have been taken from them. Jewish men convert to rid themselves of their Jewish wives. The poorest Jews convert to collect the money, the dowry, whatever prize they have been promised by the Church. The Jews turn on one another.

A woman who despises her husband's mother will swear before a notary that she overheard the woman say she would like to convert, and the mother-in-law's fate is sealed.

How he would love to greet the pope in the morning with news of the del Monte girl's salvation. What affection, what honor Benedict would heap on him! How brilliantly the baptism would be celebrated! Sonnets would be commissioned to commemorate the glorious redemption of her soul. A cavalcade would ride through the streets of the ghetto, trumpets blaring, the neophyte herself in the midst of the parade, dressed in robes of white silk. Perhaps the pope himself would insist on officiating under the blue and gold vault of the Basilica di Santa Maria sopra Minerva, or at the ancient font of the Battistero Lateranense, or even at the high altar of Saint Peter's Basilica, all this splendor and ceremony designed to encourage more Jews to convert and to display the generosity of the pope. But the girl shows no sign of relenting.

De' Rossi believes that these forced baptisms are false, the neophytes not to be trusted. The love of Jesus Christ must come freely, truly from the heart. Even the Office of the Inquisition opposes this type of coercion. The smug rector may go down for it one day. He is not invulnerable.

De' Rossi pushes himself up from his chair. It is too dark in his bedchamber to see the image of the Holy Mother Mary that hangs on the wall, but it is enough to know that she is there. He kneels on the cushioned prayer bench. *Benedictus Deus. Benedictum Nomen Sanctum eius. Blessed be God. Blessed be His holy name.* He thanks God that he was born Catholic, that for all his cynicism, he can never remember a time when he questioned the sanctity of the one, true faith. And then he begs the Mother of Christ to show him what to do with the del Monte girl. "*Dominus misereatur...* Gracious Lord, lead me to obey both my conscience and my pope."

ALL NIGHT Anna lay awake imagining what "justice" the vicegerent had in mind for her. What crime had she committed? What is the penalty for a lowly Jew who speaks brashly to a general in Christ's army? Will they hang her by the arms from the pole in Campo de' Fiori? Will they flog her? Burn her alive? What use is she to them? Savta Rachele says the Cabala teaches that judgment must be tempered by love, or it will destroy life. Anna thinks the vicegerent cannot know very much about love.

This morning, the old prioress sat beside her on the bed, and with an angelic smile, she said that Jesus Christ has been her life, that she is filled with the joy of his great light, and that his blessed mother watches over her and hears her prayers. She said that the young ones in white veils are new nuns who have not yet taken their final vows, that they are like daughters to her, the only children she has ever wanted. She said she hopes that Anna, too, will become her daughter and follow her path. She squeezed Anna's hands and kissed her forehead, and Anna felt strangely comforted by her presence until the old nun said that the thought of Anna's poor soul consigned to the inferno for eternity horrified her.

Now she has brought three more priests to the cell, three more to tell Anna that the vicegerent can keep her imprisoned as long as he likes, that it is time to accept her fate and recognize the one true light. They never come to the cell alone. Always, there are three of them—one to speak, two to look on. They try threats, flattery, promises. Anna believes that they are converts, all of them. Her refusal to fall into the arms of the Church greatly disturbs them. It forces them to ask questions they cannot afford to answer. Why have they forsaken their families, their heritage, the religion that flows like blood through their veins while she so vehemently refuses to do likewise? What are they now, but Jews disguised as Catholics?

They sit on wooden chairs staring at her, bearded men in loose robes and tight sandals. The prioress smiles sadly. Anna believes that the old woman is truly sorry for her, that she fears for her soul. But she is more able to strangle herself than to become Catholic. How many months will she remain here before they grow tired of her and leave her to rot in silence?

Now the one who speaks bends over her, his wooden beads clattering in his hand. He tells her in his kindest tones that she should think clearly and resign herself, that she will be converted either willingly or by force. He says that he wants to whisper a simple word in her ear, a word that will surely convert her.

Rage, her only friend in this place, rises to her

defense. A word! "What is this word? I have no need of your secret!"

The priest is all calm and softness. "I mean you no harm. I only wish to enlighten your mind with something that will be to your advantage." He tells the other priests to leave, and the prioress, as well. The old woman looks at Anna for a long moment before leaving her.

"I do not wish to convert you by force," he says.

They say one thing and then the opposite. She is sick of hearing it.

"No, what I will do to convert you is to offer you a wonderful marriage to a prince of high rank who is eager for a Jewish wife. I have been assigned the task of persuading you to accept his proposal, which includes a large dowry. You have only to say that you agree to convert, and from that moment, you will travel in a carriage and be served like a lady. You will be a princess."

It is the sort of lie that must work well on the poorest ghetto girls. Jews are not permitted to own carriages, and Jewish women are required to cover their heads in yellow, the same color prostitutes are compelled to wear. To ride in a carriage and be treated like a lady might be a thing worth trading for your life and your soul. The priest watches her face, smiling as though he has just given a wonderful gift to a little girl and cannot wait to see how well she likes it. Anna will tell him how well.

"You are like a diabolical spirit who has offered me a great deal of gold and precious stones, if only I will come to live with him. But in the Hebrew religion, we are taught that gold and jewels are meaningless, that when we die, we bring nothing with us to the next world but the Holy Law of God and the good works we have done in this life. Riches and material things are only temporary, but our God has promised the eternity of future life to us, the children of Abraham. So, offer the prince of high rank to some other Jewess and leave me in peace."

Anna has added another bit of eggshell to the back of the food box. So long as she is trapped in this cell, even if she spends the whole of her life here, she will still count the days.

WHEN ANNA del Monte was eight years old, she stood at the entrance to her grandparents' bedroom, tearful and afraid, clutching her sister's hand. Her father stood in a corner, draped in his fringed silk prayer shawl, weeping and praying.

The lump in the bed could not be her grandfather, not her Saba Sandro. A sheet covered everything but his head. His hair was splayed on the pillow like a crown of white feathers. His eyes were closed, the lids livid. Savta Rachele sat on the bed beside him, sobbing into her handkerchief. For three days she had refused to leave her dying husband, not even to empty the chamber pot hidden in the wall.

Anna and her sister couldn't move from the threshold, so Mammà gave them a little push. "Go now, girls. Say goodbye to your saba. He is waiting for you."

The room smelled of herbal potions, vomit, urine, and blood. Allegrezza took Anna by the hand and dragged her to the bed. Their grandmother put her arms around them.

"*Aùh*! How he loved you! How he loved you! Kiss him. Give him one last kiss."

Alessandro del Monte's cheeks were covered in scratchy white stubble. Anna bent her head down, but she couldn't bear to put her lips on the face she had kissed so many times before. She felt her grandmother's breath in her ear. How could she refuse to kiss her grandfather who loved her so much? Her grandfather who had held her and stroked her hair, who had danced and laughed with her? Her grandfather who had delighted in bringing her little gifts? She found a hairless spot just under his eye to kiss. And then she ran out of the room, down the staircase, into the street.

Neighbors standing outside their shops called out to her, but she kept running, searching wildly for her brother. She stumbled, nearly overturning a basket of fabric remnants. Tears streamed down her cheeks, dripped off her chin. She ran around corners, through alleyways into the Piazza delle Tre Cannelle. And there he was, her brother Tranquillo, sitting on the edge of the fountain, his prayer book open in his lap.

"Channà!" he called to her. "What are you doing here? You should have a jacket."

A jacket. How could he think of a jacket? "'quillo! Saba 'sandro is dead!"

"Is he? Saba 'sandro is dying."

"What does that mean? He is dead. I kissed him and his skin was cold. What will happen to him? What prayer is Tatà saying? What are you reading? Why did you leave the house?"

"*Aùh*! Channà, always with the questions. One at a time, please."

She sat beside him. His arm warmed her shoulders.

"I left the house because I wanted to be outside, Channà, under the sky. I needed to talk with our god, the God of Abraham."

"'quillo, God is everywhere."

"He *is* everywhere, *sòrèma*, but sometimes He is hard to find."

Anna looked up at the dusky sky, expecting to find God there smiling down at them, but all she saw was a black-smudged cloud. "Savta Rachele says that when Saba 'sandro dies, every good thought, every good word, every good deed of his life will become a clear light that will shine on us so long as we remember him."

"That's Savta's Cabala. Cicero said the same thing. He wrote, 'The life of the dead is placed in the memories of the living. The love he gave in life keeps a man alive beyond his time.' And Cicero said that the last day of a man's life does not bring extinction but change of place. Which means that Saba is going away. Death is the end of the soul's journey on earth but the beginning of a new journey in Olam Ha-Ba, in Gan Eden."

"Will he be happy there? Will Saba see his dead father and mother? Will he see Tatà's baby brother who died when he was only two? Will he see Savta Rachele there someday? Do you know what I think, 'quillo? I think we cannot know anything about Gan Eden until we die ourselves. It helps me to believe what I believe."

"And what do you believe, my Channà?"

"What Mammà says. Death is like birth, part of life, God's plan. 'Then Abraham breathed his last and died at a good old age, an old man and full of years; and he was gathered to his people.' That's in the Bible."

"*El malay rachamim shochen bamiromim,* say it with me, sòrèma."

"El malay rachamin, Oh Lord, God, full of compassion, who dwellest on high, grant the soul of our beloved Saba perfect rest beneath the shelter of Thy divine presence."

WHEN ANNA and her brother returned home, all the windows were open so Alessandro del Monte's soul could fly away. Mammà was pouring water from jugs and carafes into a barrel for the Angel of Death to wash his sword. When the *Chavra Chadic* society arrived to prepare the corpse for the grave, Savta Rachele threw her body over her dead husband's and was persuaded to move only after an hour of begging.

The next evening, Rabbi Mielì and the men of the Confraternità of Charity and Death walked with Benedetto and Tranquillo beside the cart that carried the last of Alessandro del Monte to the Jewish cemetery on the Aventine hill. They had no torches. They sang no prayers. They were not permitted to parade through the streets of Rome spreading their Jewishness. Women were not permitted to come to the cemetery because their sobbing and wailing might disturb the Christians who lived nearby. So, the men went silently to bury Alessandro, whom the rabbi called by his Jewish name, Moisé. After Rabbi Mielì quietly led the prayers, they hurried back in the dark. Jews are locked into the ghetto an hour after sunset, immediately after the ringing of the Ave Maria bells, and they were late. A Catholic guard had to be paid to accompany them, and another to open the gates.

THE *sorèr* demon has come back again, bringing with him another priest who is no more than a pair of watchful eyes and a silent mouth. The demon has been threatening Anna, sprinkling his water all over. He is as adamant in his will as she is in hers, and she wonders if he will be punished if he fails or rewarded if he succeeds.

Today he has decided that she must pray with him. "You will say one part in your own way, and then we will say another. Pray with all your heart as we will pray with ours. Pray to God that he may lead you to His commandments." She stares at him dumbly, and in his frustration, he grips her arm and throws her onto her knees while the prioress looks on, blank-faced.

Both priests have their eyes closed, but Anna's eyes are open. She is watching the prioress who is sitting on the hard, wooden chair, the coral beads of her rosary laced through her fingers, her hands on her lap as white and limp as a skinned fish.

The demon mumbles *Credo in Drum Patrem omnipotentem, Creatorem caeli et terrae*, and for an hour, Anna replies, *Baruch atai Adonai Eloheinu melech ha-olam*, but really, she cannot continue, because to pray with these priests is disrespectful to her religion and her god—and because this nonsense dialogue in Latin and Hebrew is so ridiculous, she can hardly keep from laughing. It only proves the impossibility of any understanding between them.

Does he imagine these methods are persuasive? This is no way to preach religion. The prioress covers her face with her pale hands. The demon's voice is calm. "Think of yourself, dear sister," he says. "If you want to be freed, you must do as I ask."

She could say again that she wants to go home, that she cannot bear to listen to another word of his preaching, but she would only be wasting her breath as he is wasting his. She sits on the floor, hugging her knees, rocking back and forth. The demon stares down at her with a look of disgust she does not see, because her eyes are closed, and her head is lowered. He steps around her as the door opens and the priests and the prioress silently follow him out of the cell, having achieved nothing.

THEY ARE two bodies with a single soul. All day she makes a Jewish home for her Gabriele and for the children to come. She is respectful to his mother and father, and they are as kind to her as they are to their own daughter. Anna cooks. She sews. She cleans. She reads. She prays. She plays the tiorba. His mother thanks God every day that her son has married such a woman. His father brings her little gifts, as Saba 'sandro used to do—a length of ribbon, a yard of brocade, a pair of enameled buttons.

No Jew will touch his wife in the presence of others, not even in the presence of his own children. But at night, Gabriele pleasures her whenever she likes. It is a wife's right and a husband's duty. She watches him as he undresses shyly, in the dark, the silhouette of his legs as he steps out of his breeches. She knows his body, his taste,

— 162 —

his smell. A man is only half alive without a wife. She has made Gabriele whole, and he has made her happy.

And now, yes! The baby moves inside her, kicks its tiny feet. Her hand covers her belly, stroking her son. Your mother loves you, *fijemo*, little one.

Gabriele Sereni with the curly dark hair, Gabriele whom she watched through the grill of the women's balcony, walks beside her through the Porta di Giudea, out of the ghetto, into the sunlight.

Iv·du et-ha·shem be·sim·chah. Serve the Lord with gladness. Come into his presence with singing.

"Anna, where has your mind gone?"

She looks up at the pale, wrinkled face of the prioress.

"I have brought you enough oil to last two hours," the old woman says. "Use the time to pray, I beg of you. Use it to ask God for guidance. Use it to save your soul."

ALLEGREZZA DEL Monte tells herself a story as she embroiders a pillowcase. She knows it may be a lie, but she tells it anyway, because she needs to believe it. In the story, Anna has been back with the family for weeks. No one remembers that she returned from the dead, and the family's attention is all on Allegrezza again. Every day they add decorations to her bridal dress—silk rosettes, satin ribbons, another bit of lace on the bodice. They speak of nothing but preparations for the wedding. Her father has hired a game master and engaged musicians for dancing. Her mother has ordered capons, cured meats, wine. Monnà Castelnuovo, her future mother-in-law, has designed an elaborate cake. The marriage contract, the *ketuba*, has been ordered from a calligrapher in Ancona who will decorate the margins with angels and flowers in Allegrezza's favorite shades of scarlet red and violet. The silversmith on the Strada della Rua has been commissioned to create a silver prayer book cover embossed with the del Monte family crest on the back and the crest of the Castelnuovo family on the front. It will be her gift to Crescenzio on the day of their wedding.

Everyone has forgotten that Anna was abducted at gun point. The image of her sister mauled by the sbirri's rough hands as they threw her into a carriage no longer haunts her and she thinks only of the room where she will live with Crescenzio, of the bed they will share.

Allegrezza tells herself the story, and then she quickly begs God for forgiveness. She is a wicked girl to think these things, but her happiness has been ruined. Everyone, even Crescenzio, has completely forgotten the wedding. They will wait for months before giving up hope that Anna will return to them, and when they finally admit she is really gone, they will grieve for her. They will cover the mirrors with black cloth and tear their clothes. It will be the same as when Saba 'sandro died, a year of mourning.

Her father does nothing now but write letters, solicit testimony, and collect signatures on petitions. Her brother barely notices her when he comes to the house.

Crescenzio is so caught up in the effort of freeing Anna, he hardly speaks to her, his intended bride. He stops by her chair and asks her how she is managing without her sister. Her mother moves through the day in a trance. Yesterday she put the clean sheets in the wash bucket and folded the soiled ones. Allegrezza does not dare to leave her alone for fear she will absently set fire to the house while lighting the *focarola*. She has had to be the strong one, the one who cooks and cleans and tends to the home. The one who gives comfort.

Sòrèma, little sister, Anna, my Channà. Where are you now? Where do you sleep? Do they give you kosher food to eat? How do you manage to keep clean there? Do they allow you to say your prayers? Allegrezza has heard stories. And if they are true? If her sister is being starved, deprived of sleep, preached at night and day? Is she being flogged for her refusal to convert? If they have managed to baptize her, no Jew will ever see her again. Channà, who held her hand wherever they went, who whispered in her ear and hid behind her skirt.

Allegrezza has ruined her embroidery. She has not made a false stitch since she was a child, but these stitches, too small to rip out and correct, are uneven and sloppy. She has wasted a perfectly good pillowcase. She wants to tear it apart, shred it into rags, but it is too precious, too hard to replace. For the rest of her life and Crescenzio's, they will sleep with this ruined pillowcase whose crooked stitches will remind them of Anna's abduction. She uses a corner of the soft fabric to dry her eyes. Allegrezza, who dares not cry for her sister, weeps for her pillowcase.

T HEY HAVE become faceless to her now, an endless parade of dark robes and sandaled feet. Words spew from their mouths like the river of foul waste that washes through the Strada della Fiumara after a heavy rain. They talk and they talk, but she is past hearing them. The one who speaks asks if she prefers heaven to hell. He says that if she does not embrace their holy faith with a good heart, she will suffer the pains of the inferno forever.

She is too tired to laugh at him. She says, "I would rather spend eternity in Hell with my honorable parents than be consigned to Heaven in the company of Catholics."

He pretends to feel sad. "Poor girl," he says. "You do not see the precipice and so you have no wish to save yourself from it."

Whatever else he says is lost to her. She never imagined that she would spend so many hours in the company of men to whom she is not related or that she would enjoy it so little. These men are Jews who have forsaken all they have ever known for the promise of a better life in the Church. If they cannot convince her of the logic of their choice, they will be forced to question it themselves, and the horror of their sacrifice will be too much for them to bear.

〜

IN THE dark of night, the old prioress has come to Anna's cell with that sorèr demon preacher. He is the worst of her tormentors, the most desperate, the cruelest. She reminds herself that he was once a Jew whose birth was celebrated by his family, a baby held in his father's arms at his circumcision, his *Brit milah*, a yeshivot boy studying the Torah. She looks at his face and tries to see him wearing a skullcap, swaying in prayer. She tries to see him kissing his mother's forehead.

"Little daughter," he begins. Every time he uses that word, "*figliola*," she wants to grab him by the beard and tear his head off.

"… you know how many times I have come here to visit you in hopes of saving you in body and soul. I have reported your obstinacy to the vicegerent, and he has commanded me to convert you today. By order of the Holy Pontiff, you will be baptized at the Sacred Font, and whether you wish it or not, you will be Catholic."

With the help of the Lord, she replies in a calm voice, "You can do as you like, but I will die as I was born. That is the truth and nothing anyone can do or say will change it."

The demon throws back his head in fury, showing his yellow teeth, his dark tongue. "Mark well the words of this obstinate Jewess," he roars at the prioress. The old woman has fear in her eyes and the red of her nose spreads over her cheeks. Her pale hands tremble in Anna's direction, then disappear into her wide sleeves.

The door closes behind them. Anna feels for the edge of the bed with her hands, lowers herself to sit. Her breath rises and falls, rises and falls. How blessed is the silence! Be calm, Channà, be calm. She must think of a prayer, a psalm to slow her breathing. Which psalm? Any psalm. The first psalm. *Happy is he who has not walked in the counsel of the wicked, nor stood in the way of sinners, nor sat in the seat of the scornful.* And ... and ... and ... *his delight is in the law of the Lord, and in His law does he meditate day and night.* Meditate. Meditate, Channà. *Schema Yisrael! Hear Ye, Israel, the Lord our God, the Lord is one. The Lord our God, the Lord is one. The Lord ...*

The opening of the door! They are back!

The demon is carrying an enormous wooden *qaròv,* a cross. Why? What will he do with this thing? Does he plan to crucify her? To beat her? "Take it away! Take it away from me!" She raises her hands, protecting her face. He paces the little cell, carrying the quaròv back and forth past the bed, from the window to the door.

"This is the hour when you must convert to our faith! This is the hour! Tonight, Jesus Christ will come to you in a dream, and so I put this cross on your bed."

Now he scurries around, sprinkling water everywhere. She cannot watch him, cannot look at the qaròv, the size of her body, on the bed. How will she sit there, sleep there? How will she bear to remain in this place? She is bent over, swaying.

She is sobbing, screaming, "It will never be! You can leave me with this piece of wood and drown me in your water. It will make no difference. If you truly loved me, you would not cause me such anguish."

The prioress leans over the bed and lifts the cross. Perhaps she pities the girl. The maggot, enraged at this, sprinkles the bed again where the cross lay, and intones a long list of their saints, Saint Cecilia, Saint Agatha, Saint Catherine of Alexandria, Saint this, Saint that.

"You will see," he says, "that tonight all these saints will visit you. They will invite you to embrace the Holy Faith, and they will cause you to call the prioress, to show her your spontaneous conversion."

WHEN DID the lamp go out? She reaches into the darkness like a blind woman. There is nothing she can touch in this miserable cell that has not been sprinkled with their putrid water, no dry place where she can sit or lay her head. Who will help her now that she no longer has the strength to help herself?

The ceiling presses down on her, the walls crush her. Her arms and legs burn with pain. She cannot swallow, not even a sip of water. She will die here. She will fast and pray until she is dead. Then she will go to Gad Eden, to the place of her ancestors, and at last, she will find peace. Her parents will know that she did not betray them, did not forsake her faith. They will throw her into unconsecrated ground where no one will ever find her. Dod Angelo will learn of her death from the vicegerent who will have to tell the memunim that she died with the name of God on her lips, the name of Adonai, Eloheinu. And that will be de' Rossi's justice, his fair treatment.

Only the dead can hear her. Only the dead souls who once loved her. *Saba 'sandro, pray for me. Welcome me. I will be with you soon.*

BELFIORE DEL Monte sits on the bed she shares with her husband. Allegrezza has finally granted her a moment of privacy. If her older daughter knocks on the door, she can lie back quickly and cover her eyes with her arm, pretending to sleep. She has taken her little jewelry casket from its hiding place behind a pile of cotton chemises and holds it open on her lap, running her hand over the smooth lacquered wood, admiring the intricate patterns embossed in the silver lid. The she opens it quickly and begins picking through the contents with her fingertips—a pair of *girandole* earrings set with brilliant-cut chrysoberyl gems, an enamel and lapis lazuli bracelet, a silver and coral hairpin, a gold pendant in the shape of a lion with a pearl body and a garnet mouth. These things found their way into the family generations ago, when the del Monte were wealthy bankers. Some were created for ancestors. Some were pawned by noblewomen with secret debts, treasures never retrieved. The bracelet was a gift from Baruch, presented at their betrothal. The earrings once belonged to her mother-in-law, Rachele, who gave them to her in honor of Tranquillo's birth. None of these pieces have any value compared with the loss of Channà. Why shouldn't she sell them now? She would have given one or the other to her younger daughter on her wedding day in any case.

Baruch must not know, and that is the problem she is trying to solve. Her husband would not be angry if he found out, but he would be humiliated. He would say that he had failed her, that she had not trusted him to defend his family. She must choose a piece that will not be noticed, a piece she rarely wears. But it must be a piece of real value. Her most precious possession is a brooch, a square-cut emerald set in intricately worked rose gold and surrounded by seed pearls. When her mother died it passed to her, the only daughter, and when her own days run out, it should rightfully pass to Allegrezza. What could a piece like this fetch? It would have to be sold to a gentile jeweler at one of the shops on the Via dei Pettinari near the Campo de' Fiori. And then, with the money, what? She could pay the lawyer Battaglia something extra for his entreaties and petitions. She could send an impressive gift to soften the heart of the vicegerent or Cardinal Ruffo who heads the Tribunal of the Inquisition.

When Belfiore was small, on a long-ago Rosh haShanah morning, her mother called her to her side. "Tell me, little one, which do you think would go well with this dress? The turquoise necklace, the coral pendant? Or should I wear this emerald brooch? Her mother held it up, smiling into the mirror. "Give me your hand, fijema. Would you like to hold the brooch for a moment? Someday, when you are a grown woman, I will be gone, and it will be yours. You must guard it well and wear it with pride. It belonged to your grandmother before it belonged to me, and to her grandmother before her."

Belfiore had never seen anything so beautiful. She held it up to the window and watched in wonder as the refracted light sparkled onto the wall and the emerald changed color from dark to radiant green. Her mother took the brooch from her little hand and put it away. It was a thing too precious to wear, a thing that might inspire envy.

She had worn the brooch twice, to Tranquillo's circumcision and to his wedding, pinned to the rose damask bodice she'd made to show it off properly. She would never dare to wear it outside the ghetto. Imagine, a Jew wearing such a thing! The Catholic sumptuary laws forbid it. So, the gem slumbered in her jewelry casket for years. It was not the joy of wearing it that meant so much, but the pleasure of knowing that she owned it. All these years, owning such a precious brooch had given her the illusion of secret wealth. She could happily wear a paste necklace to the synagogue, knowing that an emerald brooch waited for her at home.

But that was no more than pride. Wicked pride. Better to be rid of it. She would take it to her brother Angelo. It was his heritage as much as hers. If he agreed, she would ask him to sell it for her. She carefully rewrapped the brooch in its velvet covering and put it back into the casket. Then she closed her eyes and prayed for sleep. She had not slept in days.

THIS AFTERNOON, the old Curate Cachèmme, who believes he is a healer of souls, has come to examine hers again. He has no sooner settled his fat bottom on the cushioned chair when he asks, "My daughter, have you resolved to embrace the Sacred Faith?"

Is he mad? What has she done or said to make him ask such a question? She says, "From the moment I was brought here, I have been resolved to return to my honorable parents."

He is not as unnerved by her answer as she was by his question. He sits back in the chair, crosses and uncrosses his legs, coughs into his pudgy fist. "It will not be possible for you to return to the ghetto, my child. You are to be kept here for two or three quarantines of forty days, until either by force or by your own free will, you become a good Christian."

So that is what he has come to tell her. The same threat she heard from the demon preacher. It terrifies her, but she refuses to accept it. She will ask again and again to be returned to her family, even if the answer is always the same. The curate's words have turned her blood to ice, but she fills her body with breath to calm herself. Her resolve must remain greater than her fear.

"To be sure, the vicegerent is a powerful man, but I cannot believe that he would want to oppress my poor soul in that way. That would be the same as killing an innocent woman. If I am kept here for such a long time, I will die in the grace of the God of Abraham, and the vicegerent will have to answer for it when his time comes."

The curate raises a bushy white eyebrow and presses his lips together. "It pleases God that you will convert." He announces it, as though the Almighty had personally sent him instructions. "My daughter, your incarceration is no different from the unpleasant treatments a doctor performs on a patient to restore the body to health. We are trying to cure your poor sick soul, which will go to hell without salvation. Resign yourself, and you will be assured of a place in Paradise with the Sacred Fathers who have recognized the truth."

Now THE prioress has entered the cell with that *malora* sister of Sabato Coen. The curate has not stopped talking, but Anna is exhausted and hears only words, words, words. Perhaps he has not noticed that his words mean nothing to her. She does not even bother to look at him. He stands up abruptly. "My dear daughter," he says, "save your soul now while there is still time, because later, if you fail to believe, you will be condemned to the abyss of hell for your cruelty and obstinance. I beg you to think on what I have told you, and with that I will leave you."

Anna is tempted to beg him to stay, rather than face the *mamzertà* Perla Coen on her own. This Perla is a stupid woman in a fine gown. It must have been no more difficult to convince her to accept Catholicism than persuading a child to accept a sweet *biscotto*. It would be an insult to goats to say that she resembles one, but Anna can think of nothing else when she sees her. Her eyes are narrow as a goat's, her nose as long as a muzzle, her teeth big enough to chew grass and her ears long enough to twitch away flies.

"Buhlieve me, Christianity is the true faith," she says, as though she could convince Anna when both scholars and madmen have failed. She throws her arms around her and no matter how Anna struggles, Perla manages to kiss her face all over. "Heart of my heart," she says, "become a good Christian to save your soul in this world and the next, and you will gain eternal glory in Paradise." Anna thinks this goat must have heard those words so often that even she has been able to memorize them.

"Buhlieve me," she says to the prioress, pronouncing the Italian words like an ignorant urchin, "from the moment that I came to buhlieve in the True Faith, I have not had a moment's regret. The Blessed Madonna has given me a husband who wants only good for me. I live in a house full of riches with a mother-in-law who loves me like her own daughter. What greater happiness could I have? In the ghetto, I was always dreaming of escape. Now that the Madonna has shown me the True Faith, I swear that there is not an hour of the day or a moment in the night I do not thank her for it."

She tries to take Anna's hands in hers, but she is not quick enough. Anna pulls them away and places them in the pockets of her skirt, where she can feel Savta Rachele's amulet.

"I am so well, so happy," Perla says. "Better than a queen. Sòrèma, think on what you do, for when you have lost your soul, it cannot be regained. I was Jewish as you are now, but I saw that this is the true religion, and I wanted to save my soul. If you become a good Christian, I will come and visit you every day, and I will bring you my greatest affection, more than if the same blood ran through our veins."

Anna thinks that she would remain Jewish if only to avoid the tedium of Perla's daily visits. "*Fa lammèdde!*" She hisses the words between her teeth, too softly to be heard. She would like to scream, "Be quiet!" but Channà del Monte is not a rude person.

Sister Innocènza appears at the door and the Coen woman flees as though she were being chased. "Anna del Monte," the nun announces, "the vicegerent wishes to see you."

The vicegerent! He has surely come to drag her to a church where he can sprinkle water on her head and consign her to eternal misery. She thinks she will remain seated on the bed and refuse to move. Would this man who calls himself a servant of God send in priests to drag her from the cell? She has heard stories of Jewish women locked up here who became violent, women who threw things at the prioress. What would happen if she managed to break the water jug over the old woman's head? But she is too weak now, too exhausted to fight.

The prioress takes her by the hand and leads her

through the door, out of the cell and down the stone staircase where some unimaginable fate awaits her. Anna's legs tremble on the steps so that she nearly falls, and the nun puts a frail little arm around her, struggling to keep her upright.

The Great Man is waiting for her in the same parlatorio, enthroned in all his glory on an enormous armchair, his spindly legs dangling like a child's, until a lackey arrives with a footstool. He seems alarmed at the sight of her, and Anna does not wonder. Day after day, she has been tortured with endless sermons. Night after night, she has been deprived of sleep. She is nearly senseless now, barely able to stand.

He says, "My child, do not be dismayed by my visit. Here, nothing will be done to anyone by force. You see that I have left my home three times to come to you, while I have never deigned to honor with my person women who were hundreds, if not thousands of times your equal. I have granted this privilege to you more than to any other woman who has come to this Casa dei Catacumeni.

"But such obstinance in refusing to embrace our true faith! On what is it founded? Since first you came here, you have met many wise, learned men. Each day, I have sent them to you, even troubling the greatest theologian in Rome to aid in your conversion, yet you have affronted these true messengers of God by remaining intransigent. How is it that you are capable of such cruelty? My desire is only to bestow on you with my own hands the sacred water of baptism."

She is seated opposite him, staring at this little man who wields such great power. "Your Excellency," she says, her rage rising to conquer her fear, "I will die a thousand times before I forsake my holy religion. You are the master of my life, but God is the master of my soul. Most illustrious Signore, you cannot force me to say what is neither in my heart nor my mind. I have been locked in a cell for twelve days without hope of leaving. Yet I have committed no crime! Nor have I ever received improper visitors or left my home unaccompanied or sat at my window showing my face to the street. How I would love to know why I was dragged from my home like a lamb to the slaughter, and why I have been tormented day and night, denied even the fleeting peace of sleep! I beg you, if you have the will to be compassionate, free me and allow me to return to my family."

She is sure she must be a sorry sight because his mouth turns down in pity.

"Listen, my little daughter, we must work within the bounds of mercy. I have been charged with the well-being of your soul, and as I must be just, I will do my duty."

His words are kind enough, but there is such arrogance in his voice, she begins to weep in fear, and seeing this, he raises a hand, motioning to the prioress, who bends her wimpled head towards his. Whatever he says to her causes them both to fall to their knees in prayer.

They are speaking so softly that Anna cannot hear the Latin words, no matter how she tries, so she sits motionless, eyes closed to avoid the horrifying images that decorate the walls and ceiling.

~

THE RUSTLE of a hem skimming the floor makes her open her eyes. She is not sure how much time has passed, or even if she has been asleep. The prioress is beside her, her pale, sweet face turned dark and bitter.

"The time has come," she says, weeping. "You must save your soul now, before it is too late. If you fail to consent, at the moment when you are engulfed in the infernal flames, you will remember this precious chance in vain. You must think, dearest daughter, that you will spend eternity in torment. Imagine the unspeakable pain as your flesh blisters and burns, consumed by fire, the unimaginable agony that never leaves you, not even for an instant. The stench of sulphur sickens you. Your poor burned body is punctured by the pitchforks of a thousand demons until there is nothing left of you, and still, they pierce you, slice you. The heat causes your eyes to burst from your head, your teeth to fall from your mouth. There is no relief from this torture, none. No night, no day, only anguish for all eternity. Can you not understand why I beg you to save yourself? Will you break my heart by consigning yourself to such a gruesome fate? Why must you be so stubborn? Why must you be so blind?"

The old nun is clutching Anna's hands. She believes that she can terrify her with descriptions of hell. What can the girl say to her? Does she expect her to believe that Saba 'sandro and all her ancestors whose righteous souls rest in *olam ha-ba* are, instead, suffering the eternal flames of a Catholic inferno? Jews do not believe is such an unforgiving afterlife. The God of Abraham is wrathful, but he is just. He will not punish a woman for following the dictates of her religion and her heart.

~

SISTER INNOCÈNZA has led Anna back to her cell, back to the dim light and stale odors. She lingers now, shifting her weight from one foot to the other, fingering her wooden rosary beads. If Anna had the strength, she would scream at the nun, beg to be left in peace. But fear and sorrow have destroyed her. She longs to close her eyes, to sleep, to dream of her home in the ghetto, the *miqudash m'at*, the little haven.

"You are a stubborn woman, Channà del Monte," the nun says, still fingering the beads at her waist, "but you're not stupid. How easy it could be for you! You don' have t' say a word, just nod your head and I'll fetch the prioress. Think of your future. You could get outta the ghetto, go where you like. The rector will find you a nice husband if you want one. Maybe a rich man. You must want a husband. What Jew will marry you now that you been smeared with Catholic teaching? Even if yer allowed t' go back, where is it written that the sbirri won't come for you again? Why don' you see the only open path?

"No? You don' see it? If you don' wish t' marry, become a nun and live with us at the convent. You'll never find such a beautiful place in the ghetto. You can walk in the garden, embroider all day. You can read the Gospels. The mother *maestra* will instruct you for two years, then you'll take your vows in a ceremony full of singing. You'll be my sister, one of us, live out your days with kind women who only wish for peace, as you do.

"Not a word? Not yes, not no? Your face is as blank as that wall, all still and empty. I know you've got a sister. You could offer her, save her soul, and you could see her every day. Do you want t' stay in this cell all alone forever?

"Very well, Channà del Monte. I'll stay here and watch you until yer ready to speak. I can wait as long as you like. All you have t' do is lower your chin, just a little bit. Just nod. You don't have t' say one word. I will watch you do it. One, two, three ... A little nod and everything will change for you. The prioress will order a wonderful meal—roast goose, wine, anything you like. No more boiled eggs."

Anna sits on the bed, staring at nothing, too weary even to sleep. She dares not move her head up or down or even to the side. It is so heavy, so painfully balanced on her neck, yet she must not move it.

The nun says, "You're not goin' t' do it, are you? You're a *testarda*, too stubborn. You won' even nod. But why not? Just one word? One little word?"

Innocènza kneels, closes her eyes in prayer. Her Latin whispers are like the buzzing of mosquitos around Anna's face, and she no longer has the will to swat them away. When the nun rises, her eyes are damp. "May your soul rest in peace, Channà del Monte. May Christ come t' you when your soul is ready t' open t' him, and may He lift you from the depths of desperation." She makes the sign of the cross and locks the door behind her.

Anna stands at the window as the light fades, leaning against the wall to keep from falling, swaying, repeating the Schemà. *Hear ye, Israel. The Lord our God, the Lord is one. And ye shall love the Lord with all your soul and with all your heart.*

～

THE PRIORESS has brought a lamp with Anna's nightly ration of oil. The shadows of her veil and wimple drift across the wall as she places it on the table. Tears drip down her wrinkled cheeks. "I beg you. I ask only for a simple word. Is that so very much? You have the power to answer my prayers, the prayers of so many. With only one word, your soul will be saved, and you will spend eternity with God in His paradise. The saints will welcome you, shower you with their love. I beg you, please. Nod your head just once and I will hurry to send for the vicegerent who will lead you himself to the baptismal font, and you will never suffer a single moment in your life.

"My child, I have loved you since the first moment you entered this cloister. Do not leave me in misery. You are in the company of the Holy Cross, which I hope will compel you to become Catholic, as I am. If you are visited tonight by the Holy Spirit, I will be with you," she whispers. "I will not go back to the convent tonight. No. I will stay in a room just below this cell, and I will listen for you. You need only take off your slipper and tap the floor with it and, in an instant, I will come to embrace you as my daughter. You will never again know despair, for the arms of the savior will hold you all the days of your life."

LONG AGO, the lamp sputtered, drowning Anna in darkness. She is tired, too tired to fight for forty days and forty more. Whatever torment awaits her cannot be worse than the endless preaching of the clerics, the threats of the young priests who wake her over and over again. She will succumb if only to once sleep through the night.

Baruch atoi Adonai. Blessed art though oh Lord, our God. Forgive me. I have lifted my slipper to call the prioress.

In the chapel of the Convento della Santissima Annunziata, thirty-nine Jewish nuns are on their knees, praying for the soul of Anna del Monte. *Sálve Regína, máter misericórdiæ: víta, dulcédo, et spes nóstra, sálve.* Some of them murmur in Latin, some of them pray silently in Italian, and some of them secretly pray in Hebrew. *Baruch atoi adonai eloheynu melech ha'olam.*

In a cell on the ground floor of the Casa dei Catacumeni, Sister Innocènza and the prioress kneel before a low table on which they have placed two candles and a carved olive wood crucifix, the head of Jesus forlornly hanging to one side. The two women pray silently, ears alert to the tap of a slipper on the floor above their heads.

With closed eyes, the prioress sees the sweet face of Anna del Monte distorted in agony. She sees the girl writhing, naked, as a green-fleshed demon inserts a flaming torch between her legs, and she beseeches the savior to redeem this aberrant soul.

Sister Innocènza prays for forgiveness. She has failed to persuade the del Monte girl, and she is grateful that the prioress has not chastised her for it. With closed eyes, she sees the benevolent face of the Mother of Christ and feels the soft caress of absolution. Then, as though in rebuke, the despondent face of her own mother appears, and Innocènza's eyes spring open. She looks about the room, at the prioress noiselessly weeping beside her. It will be a long night, and the stone floor is cold. Her knees have already begun to ache. She wonders what she can think about to pass the time.

B ENEDICT XIV rose at dawn, spent an hour in prayer, partook of a single biscuit with a cup of chocolate, and completed his morning stroll in the gardens of the Pontifical Palace on the Quirinal hill, a stream of secretaries following at a discrete distance. As the sun burnished the rooftops of Rome, he trod the last steps of the palm-bordered path to his newly built coffee house, his Saturday retreat. But this is not a day of rest. The Pope labors incessantly, from early morning until late at night, and he complains bitterly that so much work causes him great suffering, yet he feels the responsibility of his office too profoundly to work less. Benedict XIV is abstemious in all things. Publicly, he eats little and forbears spirits of any kind, denying himself even a small glass of wine, yet he somehow manages to maintain a more than healthy corpulence.

Nine years on the papal throne have subtracted little from his simple, friendly countenance. At the age of seventy-four, he still has the plump face women long to pinch. Deep blue eyes seem to betray hidden amusement and his lips always appear to be smiling. His only concession to vanity is the quarter hour he permits his barber to spend shaving his cheeks each morning. Neglected gray curls escape his red velvet cap and straggle down his neck.

At the moment, the Pope is seated on the papal chair by a wide window in his coffeehouse where he can enjoy the calming sounds of the birds and fountains before the day's obligations besiege him. This morning, he must deal with de' Rossi, the vicegerent, who will surely bring news of the del Monte girl, another victory for the Church, another soul saved from the demon's clutches. Already, he has begun to imagine the pageant he will order to celebrate her baptism. Whenever it seems appropriate, he prefers to baptize these young women personally. It gives him great pleasure to know that another soul has been brought into the light, saved from the dark shadows of Judaism.

When he was still Prospero Lambertini, Cardinal Archbishop of Bologna, he was involved in the case of Samuele Ascoli, a newly baptized Christian still living in the Casa dei Catacumeni in Rome, who confessed that he had left a wife, Mazel-tob Olivetti, and a little son in the ghetto. The sbirri were immediately dispatched to claim them, but there was some trouble. The boy was eventually found, hidden at the home of one of the synagogue beadles, but the wife had disappeared, and she was carrying another child in her womb.

Mazel-tob, the, daughter of householder Jacob Olivetti, was eventually discovered at the home of her parents in her native town of Cento near Ferrara. As she obstinately refused to follow her husband and son into

the True Faith, the local authorities sent a Christian mid-
wife to keep watch over her in her confinement, ready
to snatch the child the moment it was born, before it
could be tainted by even a moment in its mother's arms.
It was baptized at the Basilica di San Biagio within an
hour of its birth and brought to the Casa dei Catacumeni
in Rome to join its father. But as no one there could
nurse the child, the mother had to be sent for. She had
barely arrived when the Good Lord called the child back.
Still, there was reason to rejoice because its soul had been
cleansed of all sin at the baptismal font, and a grand
choral funeral was held, with a procession that passed
through the streets of the Roman ghetto.

For a few days, the mother, too weak from childbirth and grief to be permitted to return to her home,
remained intractable. But ultimately, through persuasion
and instruction, she saw the Light of Christ.

When he heard this blessed news, the future pope
hurried from Bologna to Rome and baptized her personally. A full cavalcade surrounded the carriage as she
was carried through the streets of the ghetto and on to
the Basilica di Santa Maria sopra Minerva where he personally performed the rite in a magnificent ceremony.
Brochures were printed with descriptions and drawings,
so that all the people might rejoice in the divine miracle
that had transformed a woman possessed by demons into
an innocent, bathed in the glory of the Lord.

~

"*CAVOLO! CAVOLO! Cavolo!*"

Though Benedict XIV is a man of great gentleness,

he often succumbs to rage. He confines his expletives to the relatively benign *"cavolo,"* cabbage, but regrets even that unpopely exclamation, and has asked his rotund secretary of state, Silvio Gonzaga, to tug on his robes whenever the word escapes his lips. This morning, the efficacy of this deterrent has been minimal. Vicegerent de' Rossi is talking too much and nothing he has to say is pleasing.

"Yesterday I questioned the girl once more myself, to be absolutely sure that her soul is beyond saving."

"Ah, de' Rossi! Such a pity, such a pity! Such a tragic loss. Perhaps the girl believes that her family is more powerful than it is. She has seen little beyond the ghetto if she has seen anything at all. The parents, what are they? They are interesting to us only in that they can cause trouble. *Beh*, I suppose that is reason enough. If, as you say, she is obstinate in her perdition and there is no reasonable hope of conversion, then we must conclude that we have failed her and return her to the ghetto. How it pains me, de' Rossi! What can be done? We have sent the best minds to reason with her, but finally, you see, it is not a question of reasoning.

"If I did not believe in our faith so strongly, I would never try to convince another man of the truth in it. I am able to wear these robes and do this work only because I believe in my soul that God has placed me here to do it. I am so happy when I can be useful to our sacred religion. Perhaps if we were to send the abbot back to speak with her again ... if she is, as you say, an exceptionally intelligent girl ... oh, *cavalo, cavolo, cavolo!*

"For the love of God, Gonzaga, stop pulling my robes! You know, de' Rossi, it is the opinion of many that a woman can be too intelligent, but I do not follow that line of thinking. Gonzaga, you agree me with on this, do you not? I have always been fascinated by intelligent and learned women. They are worth quite as much as men when it comes to study.

"This young woman will not be persuaded by reason because she chooses not to be. To fail to see the Light of Christ when it has been plainly shown is a choice. So, what are we to do with her? This is what I find so difficult to understand. How is it possible that a woman with such a good mind is clearly shown the truth by the greatest theologians in Rome, yet refuses to see it? I fear that her false religion has been so deeply impressed on her, she has been blinded to anything else. Will a dog who has been fed only offal refuse to eat steak when it is offered to him? This is our challenge, de' Rossi.

"What horrors may await her in the next world? The poor child. What horrors! It is a struggle of one set of strongly held beliefs against another. God has challenged us to change the mind and heart of the girl, to prove that her beliefs are wrong and that ours are the correct ones. The only correct ones. And we have failed in our duty. Christ died for all men, even those who refuse to see Him when He is clearly shown to them. Saint James taught us that Christ is the way, not one way among many, but the only way in which a soul is saved from sin."

The pope purses his plump lips and holds the vicegerent's eyes for a moment. "Now, what to do with this Jewess? If she remains obstinate, and we see no signs whatever that she will relent, then we must send her home as you argued, de' Rossi. But how it pains me, how it pains me! If she is as bright and learned as you say, what an example she could have been! What a fine Catholic she would have made! How well she could use her intelligence in the service of the Lord! Perhaps we need not despair so soon. You must think on it, de' Rossi. I leave the girl entirely in your hands."

THE VICEGERENT's carriage rolls down the Quirinal hill, its only passenger leaning back against the padded leather seat, eyes closed, deep in prayer. He begs Christ the Savior to give him the will and the strength to do what he must do. Christ teaches us to love our fellow men as we love ourselves. That is Christianity as he understands it. Perhaps the souls of the infidels will all burn in hell when they die, but he cannot see how that justifies tormenting them while they still live. It has not always been easy to reconcile canonic law with the dictates of his conscience, but he is comforted by the knowledge that he has never broken his vow of obedience, and he reminds himself that the red cap of a cardinal has never been placed on the head of a recalcitrant archbishop.

Two years before, a Hebrew grandfather, the oldest living male and head of his family, chose to convert to the One True Faith. He was close to the end of his life and could already feel the flames of hell reaching for his unrepentant soul. After his baptism, wishing to save the souls of his descendants, he offered both his son's children to the Church. According to the Pope's dictates, he had every right to do so. De' Rossi was obligated to send the sbirri to the ghetto in the dark of night to avoid setting off a riot and to seize the children from their parents. The governors of the ghetto came to see him. They told him of the terrified screams of the children, the desperate pleas of the weeping father and mother. They described the sound of crying and wailing in such a compelling manner the vicegerent fancied he could hear it. There was nothing he could do. The law is the law and he had merely obeyed it.

But the sound of screaming children deprives him of sleep, prevents him from digesting his food. When he interviewed the children in the care of the nuns at the Casa dei Catacumeni, they seemed healthy enough. But were they? They were baptized and placed with good Catholic families. Three of them were so young, they must have forgotten their own parents. But had they?

The boy was seven, the age of reason according to canonic law, old enough to know his own mind. But his sister was only five years of age. When he asked her if she would like to become a Catholic, she nodded her little head at once, and said, "Yes, Monseigneur." The eyes of that cunning Rector Mileti were on her. How could he be sure she had not answered out of fear?

The old grandfather was not satisfied. He offered the next child his daughter-in-law conceived, even while she carried it in her womb. The Hebrew governors sent a letter arguing that it reflected badly on the Catholic religion, that it deprived the Jews of their God-given right to bear fruit. The poor parents, having lost two children to the Church, lost a third to the grave, or so they said. In any case, a funeral was held. The rector accused them of smuggling the baby out of the ghetto. De' Rossi hoped they had.

A reasonable Jew who is shown the true religion should always recognize it. It should be a simple matter of education, of explanation. De' Rossi finds it difficult to understand why this is not the case, why so many conversions must be coerced. The del Monte girl appears so pale, so exhausted. Why should learning to love Jesus involve suffering?

He knows that the rector and his rabid Dominicans have extracted too many false conversions, but he keeps that knowledge to himself. No one dares disillusion the pope, who rejoices at every baptism. If the del Monte girl remains locked in the Casa dei Catacumeni for weeks, months, eventually she will relent, and the jubilant pope will reward him well for his steadfastness. But the important ghetto families will be enraged. Who knows what resistance, what disobedience he will have to overcome? If he releases the girl, those families will owe him their extreme gratitude.

The pope will not even try to hide his disappointment. There will be no rewards, no favors, no warm greetings on Wednesdays and Saturdays. The cardinals may no longer feel the need to acknowledge him when he passes them in the corridors of the Vatican.

De' Rossi's back pains him. His stomach churns. He is growing old and has fought too many battles. If he does what he knows to be right, perhaps his conscience will remain silent long enough to permit him to sleep through the night. The Hebrew governors and their Catholic lawyer began petitioning the Tribunal of the Inquisition the morning after the girl was taken from her family. If the case comes before them, the court will decide in favor of the Jews because the claim of betrothal is clearly false. The del Monte father has collected more than fifty signatures disputing Sabato Coen's sworn statement. And de' Rossi has heard rumors that one of the cardinals who sits on the Tribunal has already been persuaded by the Jews who have somehow imperiled his secrets, touched his heart, or filled his pockets. But these trials take time, and the girl may well relent before a verdict is decided. She may even die. She looked so unwell it alarmed him.

The carriage slows as it reaches the residence on the Piazza della Colonna. The vicegerent sits up straighter, pulls the lace cuffs from the sleeves of his abitocorto, adjusts his hat over his wig. The coachmen jump down to open the door. De' Rossi places one high-heeled pump on the top step, then another. Deacon Amati steps out of the porte cochère and offers a hand, a question dancing on his lips. "Yes, I found the pope to be quite well," de' Rossi answers, telling him nothing. "It was a good interview." He hands the deacon his hat and walking stick, his leather portfolio. "Ask Claudio to come to my study and to bring the brandy. The meal can wait. In half an hour I will have a missive for Rector Mileti, and I will ask you to see that the prayer book belonging to the Marchesa Falconieri-Albertoni is returned to her."

IN HER dream, Anna saw her grandfather dressed in an exquisitely tailored black frock coat, and on his head, the yellow hat Jews must wear outside the ghetto. He said, "Channà, I am working with all your ancestors to help you. Be true to our God and keep the Schemà Yisrael on your lips. You will only have to suffer a little more." With tears in her eyes, she called to him. "Saba, when will I be free of this torment?" "Soon," he answered. She rushed to kiss his hand, but at that moment, she woke up in greater despair than ever before and found herself sitting on the *madètta* bed, her slipper in her lap. And as dawn had arrived, she washed quickly and began to pray with all her heart.

4TH OF MAY, 1749 (16TH OF IYAR, 5509)
SUNDAY (IOM RISHON)

T HEY HAVE not disturbed her all morning. She
wonders if they have finally lost hope of saving
her soul until she counts the bits of eggshell at
the back of the food box and realizes that today is their
sabbath, their day of rest. This morning, no one will disturb her, no one will distract her from longing for the
arms of her mother and father or from the terror of living
out her days in this cell.

She has no fear of their Catholic hell. She could never
believe in anything so preposterous. She knows that the
body is buried in the ground to await the coming of the
true messiah when the dead will rise from their graves.
She has been taught that the freed soul spends a year in
Sheol, the dim Land of Forgetfulness, while male relatives and friends pray for its entry into Gan Eden, the
paradise of Adam and Eve, and she has never questioned
the truth of it. These Catholics cannot threaten her with
their colorful tales of the Inferno. Her soul is safe within

her where God placed it when she was born, where it will remain until she dies, and nothing anyone says can change that.

There are thirteen bits of eggshell at the back of the food box. She touches them carefully, afraid of breaking one and losing count. She can have no thought of leaving this place until there are forty. Twenty-seven days more.

All morning, she recites the psalms, walking back and forth in the little cell until the sun no longer leaves a shadow on the ancient wall outside the window. With every syllable, every word of every psalm, the terror that strangles her day and night loosens a little. *Ledhâvidh 'êleykha Adonay naphshiy 'esâ' 'elohay bekhabhâthachtiy 'al-'êbhoshâh 'al-ya`altsu 'oyebhay liy.* Oh God, in Thee have I trusted, let me not be ashamed; let not mine enemies triumph over me.

Then one of the white-veiled nuns appears, bringing the linen she wore when they brought her here, now laundered and folded. When the nun leaves, she removes the harsh underthings the nuns have given her, and the soft cloth embraces her like a visitor from home.

Now the noon bells ring over her head and Sister Innocènza's black veil wafts behind her as she enters the cell. She presses her lips together, clasps her hands as though in prayer. "D'you ever see a woman selling buttons on the Vicolo della Torre?"

Anna nods. Everyone in the ghetto sees everyone else.

Sister Innocènza puts her finger to her lips before Anna can ask the obvious questions. Then she beckons her to follow, and they descend the stone staircase in silence.

Surely the vicegerent and the prioress are waiting to

besiege her with more admonitions, more warnings of the tortures of their Catholic hell. Anna's legs are weak from exhaustion and loneliness, made weaker still by fear. Sister Innocènza reaches out to steady her, but Anna pushes the nun away. If she is to be imprisoned in this place forever, she'd prefer to fall and break her head.

At the foot of the stairs, Innocènza disappears down a dark corridor without a word, and Anna stands alone, staring at the massive door. Two Sundays before, the sbirri hurled her through that door as she struggled against the brutal arms that constrained her. Heavy iron bars cross the old wood now, but it is a door, and the world is on the other side.

Footsteps approach from the corridor, and she stops breathing to better hear the sound, to be sure she is not imagining it. Someone is moving towards her from the shadows, a person dressed in dark clothing, and some sort of hat. A cleric. A man. She has learned to loathe them all. This one will want to convert her in his own way. Will he hang her by the arms until she begs for mercy? Will she say "yes" this time to save her life? Or will she be brave enough to resist, alert enough to remember that there is no life without her religion, her family.

Two nuns emerge behind him, one tall, the other fat, both old women like the prioress. The tall one wears a ring of keys at her waist. The bolts slide apart. The fat old nun leans against the wooden door, and it opens. Still, Anna stands at the foot of the stairs, bewildered by the light and noise that pours in from the Via dei Neofiti. The cleric turns to her. He says, "*Vieni,*" one word, without smiling, without even looking at her, just a gloved hand, a crooked finger. At first, she can't think what this means, and she is afraid to step over the threshold. She backs away a little, hands reaching for the wall behind her. The Catacumeni is a nightmare, but it is a familiar one.

"I am Deacon Amati, in the service of His Excellency the Vicegerent," the man says. And again, he gestures with his gloved hand.

She thinks she ought not trust this man who does not say where he is taking her. Then she thinks that she would follow anyone through that door, and she steps into the blinding light and deafening noise of a Roman afternoon. She lowers her head, keeps her eye on the heeled-boots of the cleric, following close behind. Should she run? Could she run? Does this man carry a pistol under his pious cloak? Are the sbirri waiting for them at the next corner? She should run now. Where would she run, a young woman alone in a soiled skirt and a wrinkled chemise? How far could she go before she was stopped by the cleric, the sbirri, a gang of street boys. She is a Jewess without the requisite yellow sciamanno covering her hair, walking in the neighborhood where Jews are hated most.

She lifts her head as she hears the splash of the Fontana di Catacumeni in the Piazza di Santa Maria de' Monti. A pair of sbirri approach, hands resting on the pistols in their belts, and she nearly falls to the ground. One of them raises a corner of his upper lip, sneering at the sight of her, but they only nod to the deacon and walk on.

She shuffles behind the cleric in her house slippers, too weak to keep up. How can she think of running? She tries to become invisible, curls her chin into her chest, hugs herself tightly, hiding her body, hoping no one will notice her. Her eyes are fixed on the cobblestones, her shoulders hunched.

The cleric stops walking.

She does not know where he has led her or if he will lead her farther. She swallows her fear and shame, forces it into the pit of her stomach. Whatever her fate may be, she must find the courage to face it. *Elohiymlânu machaseh vâ`oz.* In God we find refuge and strength.

She lifts her head, squints at the bright sunlight, at an ordinary Roman street. The noise of the city, of chatter, horses' hooves and wooden cartwheels, of shouting and laughter. Two women stroll down the Strada de' Serpenti arm in arm, heads together, whispering. A man sits on a wooden crate, repairing his shoe. Stray dogs chase each other down the hill.

And there! Oh, there! There!

She is stumbling, tripping over her skirts. She thought she hadn't the strength to run, but she is running. She leans into Dod Angelo's soft belly, buries her nose in the wool of his brown frock coat. His beard brushes her forehead. He holds her up as her legs fail her.

"Is it over? Is it over?"

His arms loosen around her. Gnòre Modigliano and gnòre Corcos, are waiting to press her hands. And behind her, the vicegerent's man waits, his face obscured by the wide brim of his hat.

He walks past them silently, and they follow. They are precisely forty rods from the Casa de' Catacumeni, a Jew is permitted to come no closer. Her thoughts are like faded ink, too blurred to decipher. She is neither awake nor dreaming. The sunlight, the noise, the smells are as astonishing to her as if she had returned from the dead.

They descend the steps of the Salita di Monte Magnanapoli to the Colonna Trajana at the foot of the hill. Her uncle turns toward the river, toward the ghetto. But the cleric raises his arm, signaling them to stop.

"His Excellency would like to see the young Jewess."

The smile has fallen from her uncle's face. His hand is on her shoulder, and she understands that this was a trick, that they are taking her somewhere to be forcibly baptized. She wants to run. She tries to shrug her uncle's hand away. He whispers, "We are here with you, Channà." And she is too weak to resist.

THEY ARE seated on an upholstered bench in a fine room with lovely book-filled shelves and a marble floor. Clergymen stand silently beside them, before them and at the doors. Dod Angelo strokes her cheek. He tells her that she is safe with him, with the memunim of the ghetto, but she is past consoling.

The endless sermons at the Catacumeni have deadened her sense of time. Perhaps they have not waited long. Perhaps they have been there all afternoon. The men exchange looks she cannot read. They sit with arms crossed and from time to time, one or another of them huffs or sighs. She wants so badly to rest, to be taken home to her bed. Her head is heavy, her limbs ache. Her breath is shallow, and she cannot stop trembling.

A bearded young cleric appears. He says, "Channà." She grasps her uncle's arm. Her stomach knots. Why has he used her Hebrew name, her ghetto name? The men stand up, but she is still seated, looking from one to the other. Her uncle pulls her up with one arm, and they prepare to follow the bearded cleric, but he says, "His Excellency wants only the girl." Anna looks at each of her three protectors. Her eyes beg them to object, to insist that she cannot be made to go alone. These are powerful men, important men, the three governors of the ghetto, yet she sees in their faces that they, too, are afraid. Afraid and enraged. Not one of them speaks. They look at her. They look at each other. And they sit down again.

It takes all her courage to follow him, but the cleric does not seem to notice. She keeps herself at a distance, too far for him to touch her but not so far that she loses sight of him. They cross a room filled with tapestries, paintings, Persian rugs, and heavy furniture. She can summon neither the strength nor the will to keep pace with this cleric. She moves slowly, grasping anything she can reach to keep from falling—the back of a chaise, the edge of a console. The cleric passes through an open door into another room where a long table is lined with gilded chairs. Jesus Christ, their mamzer, hangs on his cross wherever she looks. She thinks there must be a church somewhere in this palace, or convent cells, or a prison, that she is being led to a place to which she would never wish to go.

When they enter the fourth room, she sees the vice-gerent seated at a polished walnut table. He looks up and gestures to a chair upholstered in red silk. He says, "My Channà, I must beg your pardon. You have been treated badly, but this will never happen to another Jewess, not so long as I am vicegerent."

She is as astonished to find herself seated in a palatial room as she was to find herself locked in a barren cell.

This shriveled little man who has insulted her, threatened her, terrified her, now wants her to pardon him. She asks the God of Abraham to give her the strength to speak. Slowly, she fills her body with breath, fills her stomach, her chest, and she summons the voice of a lioness.

"I am innocent, and I was made to suffer unjustly."

She searches his face for anger but finds only sadness. "I cannot deny it, my child," he says. "Forgive me. Now go. Comfort your family. They are waiting for you."

As THEY pass through the shadow of the gate of Severus, the crazy beggar who sits there all day, reciting the Schemà, jumps up and runs through the streets screaming, "*Lei è tornata! Lei è tornata!* Channà del Monte has returned!" And every shuttered window in the ghetto opens.

Her mother and father are already in the Piazza di Giudea, both of them weeping, and when she sees them, she falls to her knees. The faces she has conjured day after day are disfigured with the pain she has caused them, and she wonders if they cry tears of relief or of shock. She knows that she is pale, that her eyes must be sunken and circled in darkness. She knows they hide what they see when they look at her.

They pull her close. They cover her face, her hands with kisses. She has longed for this, dreamed of it, but now she thinks they will never stop, and she is so tired. Allegrezza and Tranquillo move toward her shyly, as though they haven't seen her in years, not days. They press their damp cheeks to hers. Anna cannot cry a single tear. Crying requires strength, and she has none. Dod

Angelo and Ggnòre Modigliano have nearly carried her from the palace of the vicegerent to the ghetto gate.

THEIR HOME is crowded with every sort of person. Anna knows that when she enters the sitting room, their heads will swivel in search of her, but at the moment, she is not on display. Allegrezza has closed the door to their bedroom and is trying to make her look a little less frightful. She has filled a bowl with warm, soapy water and wiped the dank cell from her face and body with a damp cloth. Now she is brushing her sister's hair. Anna has asked her to braid the sides and pin them to the back of her head like Chiara, but Allegrezza says she will make her hair even prettier with ribbons woven through the braids. She has laid out Anna's best gown, deep green silk embroidered with roses. She tells her sister that she will look so lovely no one will believe she has been held at the Catacumeni for thirteen days and nights. But when she brings the mirror, Anna sees that her eyes stare out of her head and her cheeks are bloodless. She wants nothing more than to fall onto the soft pillows of their bed, into the oblivion of sleep.

The noise of chattering, laughing, celebrating invades her head. "Allegrezza, I cannot go into that room with so many people. I have been consumed body and soul. Look at me."

"I am looking," her sister says. "What do I see? A pretty girl who would be truly beautiful if she would smile."

"You cannot expect me to believe you, soremà, but

if it makes you feel better, say it. I am not the sister the sbirri dragged from our home."

Allegrezza takes both her hands. "You are tired, so tired, but these people will not leave until they get a look at you, no matter how long you hide."

"They will see a girl who is more dead than alive."

"They will see a woman who has triumphed. Now hold tightly to my hand while I open the door."

Anna nods, then pulls away. "Alle! Is Gabriele Sereni here? Walk in front of me, and if you see him, turn in a different direction so I can hide my face."

"Gabriele Sereni! You told Tatà that for thirteen days in that cell you recited psalms, but it was really the thought of Gabi Sereni that saved your soul from the goim! You funny girl!"

The door opens just enough to allow Ester to poke her grinning face into the room. "Channà? Your brother has been keeping everyone away, but you had better come out now. Tranquillo says that you are not to talk about anything tonight. They will ask you a lot of questions, but you are to say only that you are glad to be at home."

Ester slips inside and closes the door behind her. "Thanks be to God that you are here. Your brother has been driving me mad. The entire family was crazed while you were gone." She hugs Anna's waist and calls to her husband, "Tranquillo, open the door."

The noisy room is suddenly silent. Anna stands on the threshold in her best dress, feeling naked. Everyone is looking at her, as though she were an actress at the moment when the curtains part. She wonders what they see. A poor battered survivor? Or has she been contaminated, no longer the good, observant Channà? How can they be sure she has not been convinced, baptized? How can they trust a girl who has come back to them, when so many others have not? Perhaps they think that she has been released so that she can steal their children as she herself was stolen.

She sees that the old ones hang back and pretend not to look. The youngest ones stare, their mouths open. Her friends, Tranquillo's friends, Allegrezza's friends, people her age smile gently, each of them, no doubt, preparing something to say to her. But what do you say to a young woman who has come back from the dead? A woman you thought had been lost forever, never to be seen again?

Perhaps Gabriele Sereni is in the room. She tells herself she no longer cares if he is here or not, and certainly, she will not allow her eyes to search for him. Ester squeezes her waist and then lets go. Mammà is close beside her now, her mouth warm against Anna's ear. "You do not have to talk to anyone. Say you are well but very tired. We will thank each one for coming, and then talk to someone else."

"Mammà, I will know what to say."

"*Aùh*! Of course, you will. What was I thinking? My Channà is never without words."

She kisses her daughter's cheek and turns to Monnà Castelnuovo. Anna has always liked Monnà Castelnuovo. She is the mother of Allegrezza's fiancée, a kind woman who teaches Hebrew to girls at the scòla and makes the best ginetti cookies in the ghetto. Anna smiles at her as she takes her hands, but she wishes they would all go away.

∽

THEY HAD to refill the lamps twice before the last of the visitors left. It is nearly midnight, and their rooms are still full of noise, but it is their noise, their family noise, which is better, more soothing than silence. Now they can have their own meal at the old table—Mammà, Savta Rachele, Allegrezza and Crescenzio, Tranquillo and Ester. Tatà stands up to say a prayer of thanks. *Baruch atoi adonai eloheinu melech ha'olam shehakol nih'ye bidvaro.*

Anna lowers her head so that no one will see that she has finally begun to cry. Allegrezza embraces her, but Anna shrugs her off. She is ashamed that she has interrupted her father's prayer with a loud sob and struggles to squash the wail that is forcing its way out of her throat. Her eyes are closed but she can feel them all, her family, her blood, staring at their plates, trading uncomfortable glances. Allegrezza has begun to cry, too.

Savta Rachele says, "*Daihènu!* Enough praying! God already knows how grateful we are. Allegrezza, serve the caponata."

And Anna lifts her head, wiping away tears, laughing.

F OR THREE days, she has had neither the will nor the strength to leave her bed. At night, Allegrezza lies beside her, staring as though she needs to be sure her sister is really there, that she is still breathing. In the mornings, Mammà begs her to eat something. Anything. Whatever she likes. She cooks her favorite foods. "You always ask me to make stracciatella soup, Channà. Just take a sip of the broth. Just one sip." How can she tell her mother that there are eggs floating in stracciatella soup, and she cannot bear the sight of them?

"Tomorrow," she says. "I promise, Mammà. Tomorrow I will eat something. Tomorrow I will dress. You are right. I will go outside so I can feel the sun on my skin. But today, I want to sleep. One more day."

She hears Mammà's voice, Savta Rachele's voice, and she is safe.

∼

THE DOOR is opening! Anna pulls the blanket over her face, but she knows it is useless to hide. She has tried this before and the priests speak just the same. They speak louder and louder, press their lips to her ear through the blanket, soiling it with their rancid breath. She listens and waits for the noise of the one who speaks but hears nothing.

When she finds the courage to lower the blanket, Tatà is sitting on the bed. "You were screaming, my Channà."

"Did I scream? I did not hear myself scream. Are you certain?"

Mammà is standing in the doorway. A lamp has been lit, and a book is lying on the bed. Tranquillo comes into the room. He says, "The second volume of Horace's odes." He wants to talk to her about Horace, but she cannot talk about anything. Ester is with him and Allegrezza. Gentle hands touch her head. Savta Rachele is stroking her hair. How long has she been here?

She watches the mouths of her family as they lean over her, talking softly, and she sees love flowing from their lips, their words like pebbles bouncing on a stream.

O N Thursdays, the bath house beside the *stufe* is reserved for women who wish to bathe in the steam, and it is always crowded. The older women arrive looking perfectly formed. Then as they unlace their corsets they expand like rising bread and Anna looks at them in wonder, knowing that once their bodies were as slender as her own. The younger women look at each other under lowered eyelids, comparing breasts, bellies and legs, telling themselves they look at least as good as anyone else. Anna has seen more of these women than their husbands will ever see.

They begin by pouring buckets of hot water over their heads, Allegrezza, Ester, Mammà, Savta Rachele, and Anna. They use small brushes and olive oil soap to scrub first their right arms and then their left, because the right side is more important to God and so must be treated with more respect. This morning, Anna knows they are all watching her, trying to remember how she looked before she was abducted, wondering how she could have lost so much fat in less than two weeks. She can feel the bones of her ribcage as her fingers brush her skin, feel her sharp hipbones. No one acknowledges that they are all naked. They laugh and gossip as though they were nicely dressed. But this morning, Anna speaks to no one, and no one speaks to her.

Savta Rachele puts an arm around her, turns her away from the curious eyes of the other young women. "Come, Channà, Mammà is waiting with the brushes. We will scrub your back."

Allegrezza gives her a hand mirror. "Look, soremà, your cheeks have gained a little color, your eyes a little brightness."

TATÀ HAS prepared her. She is to expect the rabbi to call her name and she is to stand up from her seat in the women's gallery and give thanks in front of the entire congregation. The older women nod at her, reach over each other to squeeze her hand. The younger ones stare. The Scòla Siciliana is the same as it has always been. Ornate silver candelabras still hang from the carved wooden ceiling. Light still filters in through arched windows. The men still sit on long wooden benches to pray, or stand in the aisles, swaying. But the glorious haven she longed for so desperately is just a crowded room.

The rabbi calls the men to the bimah, one after another, to read from today's Torah portion. When Gabriele Sereni is called, she is not ashamed to put her eye to the grate, no matter that her sister has covered her mouth to keep from laughing. She watches him move towards the front of the room, adjusting his prayer shawl over his shoulders.

Something in her has died, or perhaps it is only hiding in fear, pretending to be asleep. All she sees is the boy who used to chase around with Tranquillo, the sweet boy who became an awkward youth with bad skin and an ungainly way of walking. Now he is a man, no stronger or smarter or better-looking than any of the others.

SATURDAY EVENING. The sun has set, the oil lamps have been filled, and the Temple Council has come to hear Anna's story. Every chair the family owns, most of the neighbors' chairs and both kitchen benches have been moved into the sitting room to accommodate the guests. Now the ample bottoms of the three memunim are planted on one of the benches, Crescenzio, Allegrezza, and Ester on the other. Rabbi Mielì, Mammà, and Savta Rachele have settled into the family's three armchairs. And Anna sits only a little less comfortably on a hard chair between Tatà and Tranquillo, who are each holding one of her hands.

Until now, she has been too exhausted, too weak to speak. She was interrogated so often in that ma'detta cell, she has become skilled at answering questions. She speaks numbly, her eyes tracing the faded pattern of the Turkish carpet. Mammà and Savta Rachele have not made a sound. Now and then, a sob escapes Tatà's throat or Tranquillo's. The more she speaks, the more they sob, and now she has been speaking so long the two of them have begun to sob in unison. She knows they are ashamed that they could not protect her. Her story shocks them, but to her, it is simply something that happened and is not happening now.

She takes back her hands so that Tatà and Tranquillo can search their pockets for handkerchiefs. She thinks she has given enough answers, that it is her turn to ask questions.

"Tell me who denounced me. Who offered me?" She knows the answer, but she deserves to hear the name spoken aloud. She needs to be certain who caused her suffering.

The members of the Temple Council are old men like Tatà. They glance at one another and stroke their graying beards. No one speaks. Everyone turns to Rabbi Mielì, who clears his throat, a clenched fist at his lips, and after a moment, he says, "That miserable beggar Sabato Coen, may his name be erased from the Book of Life, claimed that you were his *callà*, his bride."

Anna nods. In the convent cell, his sister, that porcheria Perla Coen, stroked her face and kissed her. She says, "I am amazed that God gave me the strength to withstand the lions who tried to steal my soul." And almost in one voice, the old men of the Temple Council murmur, shoulders swaying, *"Ho du l'adonai ki tov." O give thanks unto the Lord, for He is good, for His mercy endureth forever.*

What else can they say? What else can they think? What happens in this life happens for reasons we will never understand. If we are blessed, we thank God for it, and if we are not, we do not waste time wondering why. She did nothing to deserve the spite of Sabato Coen. Perhaps it is equally true that she did nothing to deserve her release from the Catacumeni. She thanks the God of Abraham, blessed be His name. But if there is someone else to whom she owes her freedom, she wants to know who it is.

"Why was I released? No one is ever released. How did it happen?"

Legs are crossed and uncrossed. Throats are cleared. Savta Rachele stares at her hands, and Anna is sure that she is hiding a secret. But how is that possible when her only weapons are potions and amulets?

Mammà stares at Dod Angelo. They might have conspired together. If they have sacrificed something on her behalf, she will never hear of it. Ester stares at Tranquillo with the smile of a proud wife, but he only glances up to share a look with Crescenzio who shares a look with Allegrezza. Anna's brother likes to brag of his contacts with well-placed goim. Outside the ghetto, to be sure, he is no more than any other Jew, but he will have tried to save her.

Only Tatà speaks. "My Channà, he says, "you were taken without justification. Gaspare Battaglia is a good lawyer. He presented the facts to the vicegerent and to the Tribunal of the Inquisition. Everyone who knows you signed a petition denying that you were ever the callà of Sabato Coen. The memunim wrote letters explaining the mistake, and because there were no grounds to keep you, you were released after the prescribed period. So, Channà, you see? There is justice in our world. A Jew is not without resources."

"Tatà, forgive me, but if that is the case, why is it that Devora Panzieri was never released, nor Sara Oliveri nor the Pavoncello girl? There was no justification in their cases, either. When is it ever justified that men with pistols seize a young woman from her home, or tear small children from the arms of their mothers? When, Tatà?"

Mammà and Savta Rachele are on their feet. "Who would like a nice piece of cake? A little glass of sweet wine? Yes?"

L ENGTHS OF cloth hang from pegs outside the
Zevi fabric shop on the Strada della Rua. The
more expensive wares are inside, piled on tables
or hidden in cabinets—striped silk twill from Damascus,
broadcloth from Salonica, *jardinière* velvets from Genoa.
Jews are prohibited from dealing in new things, but the
Zevi have provided fabrics to the Church and the nobil-
ity for generations. And who is to decide what is new and
what is old?

Belfiore del Monte leans on a table, fingering a
length of damask, waiting for the shop to empty while
her brother measures three meters of dark wool serge
for a gentile woman and her daughter. When the sale is
concluded, he moves to the shelves of an open cabinet
and rearranges the trays of buttons, threads, embroidery
needles. "Soremà," he says without turning to his sister,
"I could not bear to sell Mammà's emerald. You should
give it to Allegrezza next month on her wedding day. And

tell your mother-in-law that the marchesa's maid came to fetch the ivory comb. I don't know what game Rachele is playing this time, but I have money for her. She should collect it."

Belfiore neither moves nor turns her head. "Badonai, fràtèmo! What are you saying? We agreed that you would sell the emerald. Why should I ever trust you? And if our Channà had not come back to us?"

Angelo Zevi smiles. It is true, he had promised to sell the emerald. But what good would it have done? No amount of money will bring a Jewish girl back to the ghetto once the sbirri have laid their hands on her. Only the Tribunal of the Inquisition can overturn such an order. He moves a tray of pewter buttons to a higher shelf. "The important thing is that Channà is back with us," he says. "Come, sorèmà, help me choose a nice gift for her. You are looking at that piece of damask. Would she like it? Is it a good color?"

Belfiore raises neither her eyes nor her voice.

"The emerald was mine to sell. If you agree to do something, you do it, fràtèma. You cannot say one thing and do another. You are a *memuneh*! You cannot afford to believe that Jews are powerless! It is your obligation to do what you can, anything you can to protect us. All the Roman Jews, but especially your own family."

A customer, a tourist dressed like an Englishman in a red frock coat, pokes his head in the shop. Angelo bows as he moves to close the door. "*Mi dispiace, egregio signore. Siamo per chiudere.*" We are about to close. Then he says a single word in English: "Clos-ed."

Belfiore turns to discretely inspect the quality of the bindings on the Englishman's buttonholes, then picks up a remnant of blue Anatolian cotton. "Baruch believes that the petitions, the letters, the arguments of the lawyer have forced de' Rossi to return her to us. Tranquillo thinks his bribes and entreaties have persuaded the Church. They have sent Anna del Monte back to the ghetto, but they have not returned my daughter to me. I have in her place a girl with lifeless eyes."

Angelo moves towards his sister. The door is closed. No one will see them or overhear them now. "Channà was released because de' Rossi decided she was not worth keeping," he says. "Baruch knows that. Perhaps the lawyer Battaglia tells himself his efforts have had some effect. The truth is that, eventually, Anna's abduction would have been struck down by the Tribunal of the Inquisition. The pope might have insisted that she be kept longer, but de' Rossi must have persuaded him otherwise.

"It's true, she is not herself now. Who really knows what happened to her there? But she will recover. Come, sorèmà, come upstairs and I will fetch your emerald."

ALLEGREZZA DEL Monte puts a hand through Ester's arm. They are wearing their oldest shoes and have tied scarves over their hair and long aprons over their skirts. The ghetto is very small, the size of four big city blocks, but some streets are more squalid than others. As they turn right to follow the curve of the Strada della Rua, the street becomes narrower, dirtier. The young women lower their eyes, step carefully, avoiding the worst of the muck. "You are a good sister," Ester says, "but I tell you this is a mistake. Why does Channà care about a nun at

that abominable place? I am here because you asked me
to come, Alle, but I think we are crazy to do this."

A cloud of dust and dirt rises with the breeze.
Allegrezza turns her head to cough. "If it eases Channà's
mind even a little, it will be worth the few minutes we
will spend here," she says. "Again this morning, my sister
refused to move from the bed. Savta Rachele is with her
now. We are all afraid to leave her alone."

Allegrezza and Ester pass through the arch that
connects the Strada della Rua to the Piazza delle Tre
Cannelle, covering their noses against the stench of
urine. They adjust their eyes to the darkness, then squint
as they emerge into the sunlight and turn into the Vicolo
del Capocciuto. The few shops here deal in rags, threadbare and faded garments, clothing that has been passed
from wearer to wearer before it comes to its final resting
place in the ghetto where it is washed and mended for the
last time. Somewhere on these squalid streets lives a button seller whose daughter disappeared into the Catholic
Church. Someone here must know her.

The woman who answers Allegrezza's question was
once beautiful, her hair long and abundant, her eyes full
of sweetness, a splendid duplicate of Eve, a fragrant rose
flowering in a putrid swamp. She was born in the mean
room where she lives still, a life spent breathing putrid
air, eating stale bread. She has barely reached the age of
thirty, but she is old.

"I know who you are trying to find," she lisps through
missing teeth, "the *malmazzàlla* widow who used to sell
old buttons and scraps of ribbon. She had two daughters,
one disappeared, the other died in childbirth. Now every
day she begs on the street near the Cinque Scòle."

Ester nudges Allegrezza away. "How do you tell a mother who has nothing left that her daughter abandoned her to become a goi, even worse, *elohim ya'azreni,* a nun? I know what you promised Channà, but please. We will find the old woman and give her the bread and oil, but we will say nothing about the nun. Please, Alle. Better she should think both her daughters are dead."

THIS EVENING again, the del Monte rooms are filled with visitors. Even Robbi de Segni, the head rabbi of Rome, has brought a gift for Anna, a filigree silver box. All the relatives and friends are here, and Mammà has been moving among the guests with a jug of wine. Only a bride receives so many gifts. Allegrezza smiles as she passes the cakes. She slept all night with her hair tied up in rags so that today it curls prettily, and she wears her best gown of blue brocade with white lace. This should be her party. She pretends to be the perfect sister, but she does not catch Anna's eye to share one of their secret looks. Signore Corcos has brought a book of psalms with a silver cover. Dod Angelo has brought several lengths of cloth so that Anna can choose something for a new dress. Signore Modigliano has brought two silver candlesticks. The Ambron family has brought a silk fan with a pearl handle. Gabriele Sereni has arrived with his family, bringing a pair of enameled buckles for Anna's slippers. He looks at her under his long dark lashes, and she smiles. Her heart is calm, her palms dry. She wonders what he is feeling as he holds her eyes. Does he feel the warmth of an old family friend? Does he feel more? Does he expect her to feel more?

When all the others have gone, Tranquillo finds her alone in the darkened kitchen, her head on the table. "Sorèmà," he says. "What is it? Now that you are with us again, you cannot be happy? Everyone loves you. You have received such generous gifts, such beautiful things."

She does not lift her head, but her voice is sharp. "What am I to do with silver candlesticks and a filigree box? Will I take them to the home of my husband? Who will marry me now? I am tainted, scarred by their mumzer, their Messiah. Their endless words have ruined my ears. Give those things to Allegrezza. She is the callà, not me. Let her take them to her new home with Crescenzio."

"Channà, look at me, please."

She does not move. "Forgive me, 'quillo. I have no strength left. You do not know what they took from me there."

"Whatever they took, you will take it back. You are a del Monte, a Zevi. That can never be taken from you. You defeated them. Who escapes the Catecumeni? Who comes back to the ghetto? You! Only you! Why are you sitting in the dark? I have something to show you. One moment, I will light the lamp."

"No, 'quillo, please. Leave me." Her head is hidden in her folded arms. She is talking to the old wooden table. "I am just waiting for Alle to go to bed, then I will follow her."

He is pulling things from his leather bag, putting them on the table.

"What is all this? What have you brought?"

He has a fistful of sharpened goose quills, a bottle of ink, a full folio of paper.

"My Channà, tomorrow we will record what happened to you so that your children, your grandchildren and mine, and all the world will know the secrets that are hidden in the Catacumeni. We will begin with the first moment of the first day and include every detail. We must write down everything, even if you think it inconsequential. We will do this for the Hebrew Congregation. We will do this so the world will know what you have endured, so that the next Jew who is abducted will know how to behave. But we must be quick, Channà, while you still remember."

She refuses to look at him. "Badonai, fràtemo! Is it not enough that I survived thirteen days in that infernal place? If I must relive it again, if I must force myself to remember what I struggle so hard to forget, I will write it with my own hand. No one will believe me, but I will write the truth, all of it. Now go home, please. Say goodnight to Ester for me ... And leave the lamp burning."

She opens an eye. The pile of quills reminds her of a koshered goose that needs plucking. She reaches for the ink bottle, turns it around as though she is counting its eight sides. She loves these things. The deckled edges of the paper are perfectly aligned like a book without its cover. A book. She takes the top page and flattens it with her hand. It is so empty. Then she lifts her head, sits up, opens the ink bottle, chooses a quill. And she begins to write.

ONE BELL. One hour after dawn. The bed is soft with coverlets. Her sister's breath is sweet and warm. In her dream, her bed was a punishment, a wooden plank, a thin straw pallet, a rough woolen blanket. In her dream, she hurried to dress before the prioress turned the key in the lock, before the daily torments began. Asleep, she had not known where she was, and she ached for where she was not.

Baruch atoi adonoi…. Blessed art thou, oh Lord, our God, King of the Universe, who has returned the soul to its body, who allows the blind to see.

AFTERWORD

NNA DEL Monte never married, and she died at the age of forty-seven. For the rest of her life, she avoided any mention of her incarceration. When her brother asked her to give him the diary so he could make a copy for safekeeping, she turned pale and nearly fainted in his arms.

After his sister's death, Tranquillo del Monte recovered the diary and made seven copies in his meticulous penmanship. He added an elaborately illustrated frontispiece with the del Monte family crest—three mountain peaks topped by a crescent moon—and the title "ABDUCTION of my sister, Anna del Monte, held at the Casa dei Catacumeni thirteen days." He also included a poem by Rabbi Mielì, which retells Anna's story in two hundred and twenty-five rhymed verses. The whole of it, including Tranquillo's introduction, was bound in a sixteenth-century parchment cover.

The diary was not seen again for nearly two hundred years until the scholar Giuseppe Sermoneta discovered one of Tranquillo's copies in a private collection in Jerusalem. In 1989, his annotated edition of the diary was published in Italy. Sermoneta's work inspired this novel.

The diary stands as an outcry against Catholic attitudes towards the Jews, which would have served Tranquillo del Monte's purposes. For various terms between 1776 and 1802, he held the office of *memuneh,* one of three governors of the Hebrew community of Rome.

Those were terrible times for the Jews. Under the twenty-four-year reign of Pope Pius VI, Giovanni Angelo Braschi, life became almost impossible. In 1775, he issued an edict with forty-four repressive measures. Many of these, like those issued by previous popes, were routinely ignored by both Jews and Christians. But the pope's "tolerant repression," as he called it, nevertheless brought the Roman Jewish community to its knees. Twelve years later, in 1787, Tranquillo del Monte and Salomone Ambron, memunim of the ghetto, wrote to England's Jewish community explaining their dire situation and requesting asylum. They had hoped to expatriate the entire Jewish population of Rome, but the English Jews were already overburdened by a great migration from Holland, Spain, and Portugal, so their plea was refused.

The onset of the French revolution, seen as anti-papist, incited a fierce anti-French sentiment, which spilled over into anti-Semitism. The people believed that the Jews, emboldened by thoughts of Liberty, Equality, and Brotherhood, were hiding weapons for the French. In 1793, a ghetto shopkeeper was discovered selling French flags. For eight days, a mob assaulted the ghetto with rifles, clubs, and knives while the terrified Jews cowered in their homes. The cardinal vicar, the vicegerent, and the Roman senate sent soldiers to quell the riot, but it was the weaponless Jews who apparently defeated them. On the last day, as the mob, screaming *"Fuoco alli Giudi!"* set fire to the ghetto gates, the sky opened as though by divine intervention, and the city was drenched in rain.

With the French invasion of Rome in 1798, life improved for the Jews. French forces arrested Pope Pius VI and banished him to France. The ghetto gates were torn down, and the restrictive laws were abolished. But after a single golden year, the French were defeated. The pope had died in exile, but the papacy returned, in the person of Barnaba Niccolò Chiaramonti, now Pope Pius VII. The ghetto gates were rebuilt, and new, ever harsher laws were imposed.

The Jews remained confined in the ghetto for more than three centuries, from 1555 until 1870, when the pope's secular rule was finally abolished, and the Italian peninsula was reunified.

In the final battle, as the forces of the new Kingdom of Italy were about to breach the walls of Rome at Porta Pio, the general, Raffaele Cadorna, was reluctant to give the order to attack because Pope Pius IX had threatened to excommunicate any soldier who fired on Rome. So it fell to a Jew, Giacomo Segre, a commander with the fifth battalion of *bersaglieri,* to raise his sword and shout, *"Sparate!"* Shoot! A cannonball blasted through the ancient wall, and the liberation armies entered the city without opposition from the demolished forces of the Papal States.

The pope was confined behind Vatican walls.

The gates of the ghetto were opened, and the Jews were free.

For the first time in history, they had the same rights as all Italian citizens.

Two generations later in 1905, Alessandro Fortis, a Jew, was elected Prime Minister of Italy.

GLOSSARY

Note: Sequestered behind ghetto walls for centuries, the Jews developed a dialect that combined Italian with Hebrew and differed from city to city. The words annotated here are from the dialect of the Roman ghetto, known as Giudeo-Romanesco, as well as Hebrew and Italian.

abitocorto. Frock coat (Italian)
adonai. Lord, God's title (Hebrew)
amata figliuola. Beloved little daughter (Italian)
amein. Amen (Hebrew)
auditori. Secretary in the Catholic clergy (Italian)
b'adonai. Interjection "Oh, my Lord!" (dialect)
baioco. Italian currency of the era, about twenty cents (Italian)
baruccabbà. Welcome (dialect)
bargello. Police chief, sheriff (Italian)
batdoda. Cousin (Hebrew)
beh. Interjection, well (Italian)
beretta. Skullcap (Italian)
bersaglieri. Marksmen, sharp-shooters (Italian)

beth midras. Hall dedicated to the study of the Torah (Hebrew)

bimah. In a Jewish temple, a raised platform with a reading desk (Hebrew)

biscotto. Cookie (Italian)

brit milah. Circumcision (Hebrew)

buon shabbat. Good sabbath (Italian and Hebrew)

cachèmme. Wind bag, chatterer (dialect)

callà. Bride (Hebrew)

canes domini. God's dogs (Latin)

caponata. An appetizer of olives, eggplant, tomatoes, and peppers (Italian)

cavolo. Cabbage (Italian)

chaminìmmi. A slow-cooked casserole prepared for the sabbath (dialect)

chavra chadic. Burial society (Hebrew)

chaya. Life (Hebrew)

chimiangk. Amulet (dialect)

chiùsi. Not circumcised (dialect)

ciambalette. Italian donut

daihènu. Enough (Hebrew)

demonà. Elegant, refined (dialect)

dod. Uncle. (Hebrew)

donorà. Dowry, bridal chest (dialect)

durcia. Female obstinance (dialect)

Elohim ya'azreni. God help me! (Hebrew)

erev shabbat. The night before the sabbath, Friday night (Hebrew)

faraone. Gambling card game (Italian)

fa lammèdde. Shut up, be quiet (dialect)

fijemo. My son (dialect)

fijema. My daughter (dialect)

focarola. Brazier (Italian)
foetor judaicus. Jewish stench (Latin)
gabbai. Beadle, synagogue warden (Hebrew)
gad eden. Paradise, heaven (Hebrew)
gemìlut chasadim. Charitable society (Hebrew)
ginetti. Lemon-orange biscuits
gnòre. Sir, mister, short for the Italian signore (dialect)
goim. Gentile (dialect)
goishe. Having to do with gentiles (dialect)
gonif. Thief (dialect)
illustre. Illustrious (Italian)
kal. Temple, synagogue (dialect)
kasher. Jewish dietary laws. Kosher
ketuba. Marriage contract, often elaborately decorated with illustrations and calligraphy (Hebrew)
Lei è tornata. She's come back (Italian)
madett'a. Cursed (dialect)
maestra. Female teacher (Italian)
malmazzàlla. Unfortunate (dialect)
malanno e danno. Diseased and damned (Italian)
malora. Damn it (Italian)
mamzertà. Despicable woman (dialect)
matroneo. The women's section of a synagogue (Italian)
meghillà. Long story, tale (dialect)
memunin. Jewish governors of the Ghetto (dialect)
memuneh. Singular of memunim (dialect)
mikvah. Ritual bath (Hebrew)
miqudash m'at. Sanctuary, home (Hebrew)
monnà. Madame, Mrs. (dialect)
mumzer. Bastard (dialect)
neofiti. Neophyte, newly baptized (Italian)
notaio. Notary (Italian)

olam ha-ba. The coming world, the hereafter (Hebrew)

pane azzimo. Matzoh (Italian)

parashah. Weekly torah portion (Hebrew)

parlatorio. Room for receiving visitors (Italian)

Pèsechi. Passover, Jewish holiday

piano nobile. The second floor of a palazzo, quarters of a nobile family (Italian)

picciurèllo. Penis (dialect)

porcheria. From the Italian for pork products, disgusting stuff (dialect)

qaròv. Crucifix (dialect)

ragioniere. Accountant (Italian)

saba. Grandfather (Hebrew)

savta. Grandmother (Hebrew)

sbirri. Cops (Italian)

scékez. Gentile hired to light a fire on the sabbath when it is forbidden (dialect)

schemà. Jewish prayer. Hear ye Israel, the Lord our God, the Lord is One

sciamanno. Head-covering shawl or scarf (dialect)

scìneco. Piece of nothing (dialect)

scòla. Temple, school (dialect)

scudi. Silver coin (Italian)

sefirot. In the Caballah, the ways in which God the Creator became manifest (Hebrew)

senti. Listen (Italian)

shalom aleichem. Peace be with you (Hebrew)

sòrèma. My sister (dialect)

sorer. Rat, informer (dialect)

speriamo. Let's hope (Italian)

stufe. Stove (Italian)

stracciatella. Soup with egg added, making a pattern of egg white resembling rags (Italian)

stufato. Stew (Italian)

Succa. Jewish holiday, Sukkot (Hebrew)

succot. Temporary structures built in celebration of Sukkot (Hebrew)

talmùd torà. Religious school for boys (Hebrew)

tatà. Father (Hebrew)

testarda. Stubborn person (Italian)

tiorba. Plucked instrument in the lute family (Italian)

Tisha b'Av. Jewish holiday marking the destruction of the temple in Jerusalem (Hebrew)

torta salata. Savoury pie (Italian)

tarèffe. Non-kosher food (dialect)

vieni. Come, come here (Italian)

yeshivot. School of Talmudic studies (Hebrew)

zio. Uncle (Italian)

ACKNOWLEDGMENTS

This book was inspired by a conversation with my dear friend, the art historian Carolyn Valone, whose paper on the Farnese women sent me down the rabbit hole in search of a "Jewish convent" and led me to Anna del Monte's diary.

Among the numerous sources I consulted in the writing of this novel, I am most deeply indebted to Giuseppe Sermoneta's *Ratto della Signora Anna del Monte*, as well as the scholarly works of Marina Caffiero, particularly *Rubare le anime, Diario di Anna del Monte ebrea romana*; *Storia degli ebrei nell'Italia moderna*; and *Battesmi Forzata, Storie di ebrei, cristiani e convertiti nella Roma dei papi.*

For insights into the context of the diary, I am indebted to Attilo Milano's *Il ghetto di Roma: illustrazioni storiche;* Kenneth Stow's *Anna and Tranquillo, Catholic Anxiety and Jewish Protest in the Age of Revolution;* Ettore Natali's *Il ghetto di Roma,* Cecil Roth's *History of the Jews in Italy,* and Angela Groppi's *Gli abitanti del ghetto di Roma, La Descriptio Hebreorum del 1733.*

I am profoundly grateful to my fellow authors Judith Dupre, Marilyn Johnson, Cathleen Medwick, and

Esmeralda Santiago, who reviewed the book chapter by chapter, offering their encouragement and wisdom.

Heartfelt thanks to my agent, Isabelle Bleecker of Nordlyset Literary, for her steadfast belief in this book, and to the team at Monkfish Book Publishing, Paul Cohen, Susan Piperato, Anne McGrath, Colin Rolfe, and Jon Sweeney, for their enthusiasm and commitment.

JOIE DAVIDOW is a writing coach and the author of several books, including a memoir, *Marked for Life*; the nonfiction *Infusions of Healing*; a novel, *An Unofficial Marriage: A Novel about Pauline Viardot and Ivan Turgenev*; and, with Esmeralda Santiago, the editor of short-story anthologies *Las Mamis* and *Las Christmas*. In her career as a journalist, Davidow was the founder and editor of two award-winning magazines—*L.A. Style* and *Sí*—and a cofounder and editor of *L.A. Weekly* newspaper.